Old Girlfriends

Old Girlfriends

Stories

DAVID UPDIKE

St. Martin's Griffin
New York

OLD GIRLFRIENDS. Copyright © 2009 by David Updike. All rights reserved. Printed in the United States of America. For information, address St. Martin's Press, 175 Fifth Avenue, New York, N.Y. 10010.

www.stmartins.com

The Library of Congress has cataloged the hardcover edition as follows:

Updike, David.
   Old girlfriends : stories / David Updike.—1st ed.
      p.   cm.
   ISBN 978-0-312-55001-1
   1. Love stories, American. I. Title.
   PS3571.P378O43 2009
   813'.54—dc22

2009007634

ISBN 978-0-312-55002-8 (trade paperback)

First St. Martin's Griffin Edition: March 2011

10 9 8 7 6 5 4 3 2 1

For my parents,
who have always been with me,
and always will be

Contents

Acknowledgments

With thanks to Wambui and Wesley, who were also always with me through the writing of these tales; to Jin Auh and Jacqueline Ko, from the Wylie Agency, for believing in these stories, and persisting; and for Vicki Lame, of St. Martin's Press, for editing them with a sure and gentle touch. Also thanks to Dorothy Antczak, at the Fine Arts Center in Provincetown, for inviting me there for several summers to teach and to read some of these stories for the first time and try them out on the world. And thanks to Charles Wright as well, for permission to use the beautiful last lines of his poem "Italian Days" at the end of the story "Kinds of Love."

Old Girlfriends

Geranium

He would live, the woman told him, at the back of the house, in the two small rooms which, now that one of her kids was away at college, they no longer used. As they went up the back staircase he followed a step or two behind her, so that his eyes fell on the ruffled blue and white fabric of her seersucker shorts, and below, the smooth tanned skin at the back of her knees, burnished brown by the late-summer sun.

"And sometimes we use this room, too," she was saying with a sweeping gesture of her hand, gliding through the dusty beams of sunlight that fell through the window nearby, "but you'll have this part of the house pretty much to yourself." She was neither young nor old, fortyish, halfway between his parents' age and his: her hair was a frazzled reddish brown, and her eyes a pale iridescent blue with a faint latticework of lines fanning out from the corners and dissipating on the flushed bloom of her cheeks. The rooms were small but had a beautiful view of the oaks and the lawn and the river beyond, and he knew he would take them, and live there, and through the windows he would watch the seasons changing, leaves turning yellow, then brown, and then falling, only to be covered by a blanket of snow which, melting in the warm April sun, would give way to green grass and yellow flowers before the whole lovely cycle repeated itself again.

"And there is an apartment above you, where Hope Hilliard lives, and another below that Peter Veen rents out as a studio—he's a painter. Have you met Peter? Well, he's very nice. We're having the gutters redone and the entire house painted this fall, so there might be some banging around for a while, but that should be over by Christmas."

He moved after Labor Day, and true to her word he was woken each morning by the good-natured sound of work-men going about their business—ladders clanging, buckets being dropped—their manly banter as they stood around sipping coffee in the first liquid rays of the sun. It was a beautiful fall—soft days of sunlight, leaves tumbling past his window, and beyond, ships gliding back and forth on the smooth broad belly of the river. At dusk he would walk to the end of the lawn and watch the sun set, and on his way back to the house catch occasional glimpses of domestic life within—Mrs. Charters gliding through the kitchen with an enormous salad bowl, her kindly husband washing dishes at the sink, their adolescent son procrastinating in the rooms above, pacing past the window like a caged animal.

He had always been attracted to families, drawn to the emanating warmth of domestic life, and was always cheered by the sounds that seeped under his door—someone thump-ing up the stairs, Mrs. Charters's tinkly laughter, the muffled din of familial banter. He was, in fact, between families himself—the one which produced him and the one which, in theory, he would produce, and he was also, for once, between girlfriends, a bachelor in fact as well as spirit, and perhaps in consequence his thoughts sometimes drifted toward the lan-guid figure of Mrs. Charters—"Lauren," as she suggested he call her—as she went about her daily routine: in jogging clothes when she returned, lightly sweating, from her morning run; in worn dungarees with a red kerchief wrapped around her head as she raked leaves on a Sunday afternoon; with briefcase in hand when she returned home after a day of work, selling houses to the rich. One morning he looked out the window and saw her at the end of the lawn in something like a bathrobe, her hair still wet, her head held high in a moment of contemplation so deep he could feel it a hundred yards away. And then her reverie was broken by the sound of a slamming door, and there was Mr. Veen, hands in pockets, striding toward her across the lawn: she turned and smiled, as in a movie or Victorian novel, speaking words which made Veen laugh but Michael could not hear. And then they strolled down the lawn together and disappeared into their respective sides of the house.

Mr. and Mrs. Charters were about the same age Michael's parents had been when they were last married, a decade or so before: she was as beautiful as he was handsome, and both had reached the stage, a kind of epiphany of adulthood, when, though "middle-aged," they were still capable of things spontaneous and athletic, possessed of a lingering spark of youth, a sense of themselves as vibrant sexual beings. She had turned forty the previous spring, she told him one day on the driveway, but then added, "I don't *feel* forty—not at all. I feel I could do anything, still!"

Michael's downward neighbor, Veen, was a pleasant, cheerful man who would arrive each morning before seven, announced by the crunch and crackle of gravel, and then the slamming of his door just beneath Michael's window. He would remain until almost midnight, working, presumably, on his meticulous landscapes, or on someone's tax return, by which, he had confessed, he earned his "bread and butter." He was a sturdy, kindly man with soft blue eyes and a beard on the verge of turning gray. And although he was friendly, and eager that he and Michael "get to know each other," he always seemed to be walking backward, away from him, as if anxious to get back inside and out of sight. Another thing Michael never understood: why he never had paint on his hands. One day he asked.

"Well, you're not supposed to, are you? I guess it's left over from my banking days—neatness. Plus, toxins—that paint has lead in it: I need all the brain cells I have left!" He looked tired, as though he had thought too much and slept too little, and was turning to go when, almost as an afterthought, he said, "Gee, Michael—do you know how free you are? No kids, no house, no college loans to pay. You could pick up right now and move to China if you wanted."

"And do what in China?"

"Whatever—live! But I can't do it—not without affecting the lives of other people—my wife, my kids—defaulting on the house." He seemed to be working toward some sort of confession, then retreated. "But I guess the grass is always greener, and all that stuff—every sword has two edges. Ah, well, too much philosophy for this early in the morning. It's nice to have you around," he added with a faint smile, and walked slowly across the driveway and into his rooms.

A few nights later Michael returned to the house to find the driveway filled with cars and the house surrounded by loitering teenagers, and on his way upstairs he ran into Mrs. Charters as she hovered upstairs, superintending from a distance this party thrown by her son.

"Do you think it's all right?" she said. "We told them they could drink, but they can't drive home. We have car pools—only the sober ones can drive." She was wearing a black evening dress and her hair fell in wispy strands down her neck, and she seemed giddy as she peered down into the room of teeming teenagers. "Do you want a beer, Michael?" she asked, and before he could answer she called down to an idle redhead who seemed relieved to have something to do and bounded up the stairs with a Rolling Rock.

"Thanks, John," she said, and ruffled up his hair. She was the kind of mother one loved doing favors for.

As Michael stood and sipped his beer, she bummed a cigarette from a girl and coolly, calmly smoked, and somehow got started talking about marriage. "I mean, in the sixties," she said, "it was wild. Tom and I were your age—younger, really—and we all had children—two, three, four. We would just bring them along to parties. They would just sleep through it. And later," she said, her voice lowered to a whisper as she glanced over her shoulder, "we were all having *affairs*. We almost divorced—I left for a week, but I couldn't stand being away from the kids. And, of course, I still loved Tom. It was different back then. We were just kids." She was interrupted by the sound of something crashing below, and suddenly clutched Michael's arm. "I have to go down," she said. Michael watched as she glided down the carpeted stairs, and then, his beer finished, he snuck back to his room.

That winter he worked at night and would get home after ten, stepping in through the side gate and crunching across the frozen snow, and would sometimes catch glimpses of Mr. and Mrs. Charters as they went about their ablutions upstairs. One breathless moonlit night he paused under a canopy of bluish stars, then hid in the shadow of an enormous oak to watch as Mrs. Charters, framed in a lit window, exchanged one garment for another, arms raised high above her as her dress fell away and a diaphanous nightgown collapsed around her like a parachute. He was too far to really see but, from his shadowy lair, was moved, and shivered both with the cold and with this pale intimation of nudity.

Spring finally came, and after a year of bachelorhood— the longest he had gone without a girlfriend since high school—he became friends with a pretty Indian woman named Sashi who taught bilingual education in a nearby town. Their courtship was mercifully brief: they kissed on the second date, and made love on the third, and soon thereafter she was spending weekends at his house, sleeping late, reading in bed, taking long walks through the quiet, blooming streets of the town. He was overwhelmed that April by the lushness of the place—the deep green lawn, yellow forsythia bush, purple lilacs, flowers that sprouted from the damp earth.

"It's beautiful, isn't it?" Mrs. Charters said one morning, surprising him when he returned from town on a bicycle with a quart of milk. She stood up from the dewy flower bed where she was working, her face flushed from her exertions. She was wearing her gym clothes, and her small pale hands had been stained brown by the loamy earth; her face was flushed, and beads of sweat clung to her skin like dew. "We planted all this last fall, but we had no idea it would look like this. By the way, Sashi is wonderful! We had a conversation the other morning—and she really is very beautiful."

Just then a door slammed, and Veen came bounding out of his apartment wearing overalls and new work gloves. "Good morning, Michael!" he all but shouted. "Are you a gardener too?"

"No, not really," he answered, but Veen didn't seem to hear him: he was already hard at work, kneeling among the weeds, nattering away to Mrs. Charters. Michael said goodbye to her and slipped inside.

"Now, why is Veen gardening with her?" Michael asked Sashi later, peering out the window to the garden, where the two had spent the better part of the morning. "And where is Mr. Charters?" Sashi was lying in bed, reading a week-old copy of the *Delhi Times*.

"Maybe he doesn't like gardening," she proposed, in her soft, mellifluous voice.

"Maybe he doesn't like Veen—I wouldn't if she were my wife."

"Luckily, she's not."

"And what does he mean by 'free, free'? A couple of months ago he gave me this big spiel about how free I was, and could do anything—fly off to China if I wanted. And do what there? And what is he so shackled for if he spends eighteen hours a day down here painting? I wonder what his wife thinks."

"Oh, leave the poor man alone—he's probably having a midlife crisis."

"And I'm going to have a pre-midlife crisis if he keeps slamming the door every morning."

"He slams the door? I never hear it."

"And then stomps around afterward in case that doesn't work."

It was on one of those mornings that, by chance, Michael looked out the window in time to see a peculiar thing: Veen, at the far end of the lawn, crouching down into the garden, lightly plucking a red rose from among the flowers, and, holding it gently between two fingers, sprinting across the lawn with it, almost on tiptoe, to the other side of the house and the Charterses' back door. Later that day he looked for signs of the rose in the window, but it was nowhere to be seen.

"They're probably just friends," Sashi said.

"Yes—the kind of friends you give roses to. And why was he half running?"

"Hmm . . . ," she said returning to her book. "What do you care, anyway?" She was naked under the mountain of covers, giving off the languorous aura of a woman made recently love to. "I think you're just jealous, because you wanted her for yourself."

"Perhaps—briefly, before we met. But that's no excuse for him—they're both married."

"So—maybe they're unhappy. In India, it's quite acceptable for a man to have an affair, as long as he's discreet about it."

"And what about a married woman?"

"Less acceptable," she said, climbing out of the bed and stretching in the sunlight, her wonderfully naked body rising before him. "Sometimes they light them on fire."

"Be careful, they'll see you," he said.

"So let them. I have nothing to hide," she said with a sly smile, and went off to shower.

It was true—he had no real case against them: only the rose, and the morning in the garden, and the rambling speech about being free. But Michael was finely attuned to the signs and signals of infidelity, having observed through the tinted glass of childhood the symptoms of his own parents' transgressions, and witnessed, after his father had taken up with another woman, the evolution of his mother's "friendship" with Mr. Thorn—spontaneous visits to borrow a ladder or return a saw, a hurried cup of tea, the flushed cheeks and whispered words as they sat together at the kitchen table, the hurried walk back across the yard and the cloud of dust his car left in parting, the distant growl of its little engine settling down across the yard. In Veen, in particular, he thought he picked up the scent of emotional distress.

Spring faded slowly and summer swelled up from the south, the high arching oaks filled with leaves that made soft lowing sounds at night, and thunderstorms rolled up the river and violently broke over the house, cracking and thundering and drenching all in sheets of rain before moving on, leaving the house and the garden a glistening sodden paradise. For a month they had gone away to his mother's house, and when they returned the lush green lawn had turned brown, and the leaves had begun to fade and fall under an amber August sun.

From his window, Michael thought Veen looked invigorated, happy, and his suspicions were confirmed when he met him one afternoon in the drive. "I like the fall—get back to work, paint a few pictures; no taxes to do. Cool night, warm days." Mrs. Charters's beauty had turned up a notch, heightened by a tan and perhaps by a new job she had taken up in a neighboring town. Rather than spying, Michael was trying to think of other things: his relationship with Sashi, for example, had continued its inexorable course, and to his private astonishment they now spoke of marriage as something natural and inevitable. Although he had long since lost his appetite for bachelorhood, his capacity to endure lonely nights at home, he was reluctant to part with his sense of himself as a roving, predatory being, and could not quite accept the notion, sweet as their lovemaking was, that Sashi would be the last woman he would ever sleep with. He had even shared his anxieties with her, but they didn't seem to faze her: "I mean, it's not ideal, is it?" she had said. "But people are people. It doesn't mean you have to destroy a marriage because you got into somebody else's knickers. Americans are so silly that way—one affair and it's all over. And who knows," she said, with her sly smile again, "it could be me who transgresses!"

And so he slowly adjusted to the sight of her belongings intermingling themselves with his—a bra joining his pajamas on a bathroom hook, a pair of high heels next to his muddy boots, bottles of perfume and other agents of female enhancement. He tried to prove himself in small, domestic ways—cooking, doing laundry, taking her to dinner and always paying the bill himself—concessions to commitment he had hitherto resisted. He sometimes wondered if being with her, a woman from a different country and culture, was liberating for both of them, had released them from the patterns and expectations of their own, released them to live in a world of their own choosing.

He had almost entirely forgotten about Veen when, one morning while scrubbing the coffeepot at the sink, he happened to glance out the window as Mrs. Charters, dressed for work, walked out onto the driveway to her car; she opened the door, there was the bang, and there came Veen, hands in pockets, springing out to speak with her. There was something in the way they stood, in the way she kept stalling getting into the car, and the way that, when she did, she rolled down her window, talked some more, gave a little wave and drove off, that rekindled his interest; thereafter, every morning at twenty to eight when he heard the door slamming he would rush to his window, look through the leaves of his wilting geranium as the whole "spontaneous" event reenacted itself, and she drove off with her little wave.

He continued his habit of responding to the door-slamming noise with a counter thump of his own, but Veen seemed not to notice. But he did half complain about the sound of him pacing around above him: "Geesh, Mike, what are you wearing up there, hobnailed boots? It sounds like Sherman's army." When had he started to call him Mike?

"I did it to keep you alert—awake—over your canvases and tax returns."

Veen chuckled. "We'd love to have you over sometime, you and Sashi, as soon as the quarter's over."

Who was "we," he wondered, then said, "Great, just let us know when." He had met Veen's wife only once. And although he felt somewhat chastened by the invitation, he could not help noticing that on Thursdays—the day Mrs. Charters told him was her day off—neither her car nor Veen's could be seen in the driveway.

"You're like an old lady!" Sashi admonished. "Why do you even care?"

"I'm not sure. . . . They're about the same age my parents were when they split up, and maybe I . . ."

"Poor baby! You survived, didn't you?"

"Yes, but scarred for life."

"Scarred, maybe, but not scared," she joked, returning to her book. "Let them be."

A few mornings later, while sleepily consuming a bowl of cornflakes, the milk so cold it made his teeth ache, he heard Veen's car crunch onto the drive and then the screen door slammed so hard it made the windows rattle. He waited a moment, then stood up, made a little jump, and came down hard on the heels of his "hobnailed" boots.

"What was that?" Sashi asked sleepily from the bed.

"Counterterrorism," he said, and a moment later the phone rang: it was Veen, asking if he was okay.

"Oh, sorry—I dropped a box of books. Moving stuff around."

"Just checking," said Veen, and Michael hung up, chastened.

"Who was that?" Sashi asked from the other room.

"Wrong number," he said—his second lie in thirty seconds. He would have to stop. It was not Veen's fault that he had fallen in love with Mrs. Charters; he might have himself if Sashi had not appeared first and saved him. Even then, what would he have done if the opportunity had arisen, say, to kiss her? He had never been adept at seducing women, but prided himself on being an opportunist, being willing and able when opportunity arose, offered up by the gods of romance and desire. What did one do with such offerings, he wondered, when one was married, the double weight of church and state weighing down upon one? They planned to go to India in the summer, and their visit would be greatly simplified if they were, in principle, engaged.

"And you will have to write to my family," Sashi said, "and make clear your intentions."

"Which intentions?"

"Exactly—you have to figure that out. Or don't write them," she said, rising to the bait, "and I'll just stay in India after our visit and you come back here." He felt like a man in a small boat on a river with no oars; in the distance, he could hear the approaching rumble of the falls.

Such were his preoccupations in those brief, lightless days before Christmas that he almost forgot about the party, until Veen called him one morning to remind him. "An annual thing," he said, "eggnog, smoked ham—the whole ball of wax. We weren't going to do it this year, but my friends kept calling and asking if we were having it. The world wants you to keep being who they think you are. I hope you both can make it."

"What should I wear?" Sashi asked on the afternoon of the party, pacing in a bra and rose-colored slip, pressed outward by her swelling hips. The closet was now filled with her fine clothes, crowding out his own.

"Something festive—maybe a sari? Do you think *she'll* be there?" he asked, but she either did not hear or ignored him, instead put on a long black dress and a string of plastic pearls in which she looked, he had to admit, ravishing. He put a tie on under his V-necked sweater, a pair of gray, seldom worn trousers, and together they walked to Veen's in the clear cold stillness of a winter night. Above them the stars seemed to turn slowly on their axis. From a block away they could hear the murmur of the party, and then they saw the house giving off its cheerful holiday glow, and as they approached, arm in arm, he had a premonition of approaching an altar.

"You made it!" Veen greeted them at the door, bending over to kiss Sashi on the cheek, and introduced them to his wife, a short, older woman who seemed more cheerful than he had expected. "Come in, come in!" she said, and they did, wading through a sea of married people to the drinks, where he poured an eggnog for Sashi and one for himself. When he turned around she was already under cross-examination by an eager-looking couple inflicting the usual barrage of questions—where she was from and what she was doing here and where she had learned such good and lovely English.

"India," she answered icily. "That's what we speak there."

"Of course! How stupid of me," the woman said, and Michael drifted away to the food table, where he partook of a delicious salty ham and some olives, then went into a tiny kid's room where the Grinch, perched high on a sleigh laden with presents, was teetering on the edge of an enormous snowdrift which would soon collapse, sending him with all his gifts cascading down the mountain into a moonlit village full of sleeping children. He turned back into the room, where he hoped to find Mrs. Charters to spice things up.

Sashi was trapped on the couch with an ardent young man who had not learned, apparently, of him, her boyfriend, and was listing hopefully toward her with his legs crossed, nodding attentively as Sashi talked, basking in the glow of male hopefulness. He did not want to join them, or intrude, so he turned back into the party, into Veen, working the crowd, a born host.

"Well, well—I always wanted to see you wearing a tie— looks good. You must find these old folks kind of dull, but can't be helped. Most of these people I've known for twenty years—or more! It was great you could come, anyway—we don't see nearly enough of each other—though I hear you a lot, those boots!"

"I hear you too," he offered, "your screen door. I always know if you're coming or going." Veen did not pick up on his secret meaning; his hand landed briefly on Michael's shoulder like a bird of prey, as Michael studied the pale, freckled back of a woman who had appeared nearby. He did not recognize her hair, and it wasn't until she turned and smiled that he knew it was Mrs. Charters. "There you both are!" she said, happily, offering herself to be hugged. Veen was beaming.

"Where is your lovely girlfriend?"

"On the couch, talking to some . . . man!" he said, feigning jealousy.

"Not to worry. She's crazy about you—it's obvious." Whether from the eggnog, or the winter cold, or her own happiness, her cheeks were flushed pink and her hair fell in frazzled wisps around her neck. She wore no necklace, leaving the snowy contours of her upper bust, descending into satin, to be considered on their own merits.

"She's quite a woman," Veen said to him.

"Sashi?"

He chuckled. "Well, both, but yes, Sashi."

"She's lovely," said Mrs. Charters, lowering her voice and leaning toward him. "Do you think you two will ever get married?"

"Gulp . . . married?" he said in mock alarm. "Well, maybe. We're going to India this summer, and we—I—will have to let be known my 'intentions.'"

"Really," said Veen thoughtfully. "I didn't know you were that type."

"Oh, well. I wilt when I'm alone, after a while."

"You know," Mrs. Charters said, glancing back and forth between the two of them, "you two are really very much alike."

"Really," Michael said, "so many compliments." They all smiled, and then she said to Veen, as if she had just remembered, reaching out to touch his forearm, "Tom was awfully sorry he couldn't come. He had his own party at the office— but I couldn't bear to go—so dull!!" The explanation, Michael knew, was for his benefit, not Veen's.

And then she bummed a cigarette from someone named Ginny, Veen refilled his eggnog and then Michael's, and as they talked, laughing and drinking and feeling, for once, at ease, some other part of him looked out through the swirling smoke, the fragrance of pine from the nearby tree, the strains of a Christmas carol some jolly soul was beginning to play and sing at the piano, and in some deep and silent space before him he saw them standing together in the amber light, each looking healthy and happy, vulnerable and hopeful, younger than he always thought of them. And there was a moment when the conversation paused, and they continued to stand there anyway, smiling, and for an instant it seemed they were offering themselves up to him, shyly and silently confessing, revealing to him their love and asking for his blessing. He knew; they knew he knew; and in the sharing of this secret he could see they were relieved of a great and unseen burden.

Sashi finally stood up, coolly escaped her hopeful fop, exchanged pleasantries with Veen and Mrs. Charters, then looped her arm through Michael's, a public statement of affiliation. And as they stood there talking, something finally left him, and he could feel himself smiling back, all four smiling, and for once he saw the beauty and sadness of their love, the loneliness of circumstance, the hardship of things to come. He could see, too, that they had wanted him to know all along: all love needs an audience, and he had become theirs. Without his even knowing, they had adopted him their son.

In the Age of Convertibles

A blue Fairlane, a lime green Mustang, a gray Corvair: back then we always had convertibles, and in the summer the roof was always open and we kids—brother, sisters, a few cousins, and I—were always in the backseat, standing up on our dirty bare feet, eyes watering, scalps tingling, wind whipping our hair as we sped along toward the beach or ice-cream store, shouting and laughing in the warm summer wind. It was the sixties, after all, and my uncle Herman had gotten rich on the stock market and wore purple plastic beads and floral printed shirts, his hair hanging in a wispy curtain from his tanned and balding head. My own father was thin, and young: he played kickball with us in the backyard and picked up hitchhikers on the way to the beach, and in the parking lot there he would throw a tennis ball high into the air above the car, then speed across the parking lot in the Corvair in time to catch it with a triumphant, upraised arm.

But by the late sixties Corvairs had all but vanished from the roads, a victim of Ralph Nader and a rear-mounted engine, so that, in the event of a collision, my father happily described, the front end crumpled "like an accordion." True enough, as it turned out, for it was just such a collision that had ended our own Corvair—my father at the wheel, a snowy road at nighttime, a cocktail party they were returning from, a curve, a skid, a telephone pole that cracked, but did not break, on impact. No one was badly hurt, but the woman who was in the front seat with my father—who was not, strangely, my mother—turned her ankle, and had to be taken to the hospital for X-rays. The Corvair was totaled, replaced, in time, by a blue Ford Fairlane, also a convertible.

The house to which we moved when I was thirteen included on its seven acres a small white cottage, inhabited by a tall, foppish young man, a graduate student in music who fell in with my parents' crowd and lent to their volleyball games and cocktail parties a certain youthful energy, and caused several of the women—divorced, or en route—to fall in love with him. My older sister, Lila, claimed she saw one of these flirtations consummated through the inadequately drawn blinds of the cottage. He, too, drove a convertible, a dented, beat-up Volkswagen Bug in which he would buzz around the driveway at all hours of the day and night on his way to and from his musical and romantic appointments. But his own car was often broken, and so it was that one night, as he was driving my father's borrowed blue Fairlane home from the city, he missed the Webster exit, came blundering up on the median strip, and bounded along for a while before coming to a smoky stop on the grass: the outside of the car was unscathed, but the underside had been disemboweled, and the car was totaled. The composer, we speculated, was drunk or had fallen asleep at the wheel, or both, but my father took it well and worked out reimbursement, and within a year the composer had moved, still driving his dented VW Bug, and in it carried the minister's wife back with him to Ohio whence he had come.

It was about this time that the marriages of my parents' friends began to disintegrate, or implode, or fizzle out to the sound of crashing plates and slamming doors and the muffled, whimpering protests of their children. My own parents' marriage seemed to hold up under the high winds of nuptial dissolution as their fellow couples split up, or moved, or recoupled with each other in surprising, unexpected ways. But then, at the beginning of the summer I turned sixteen, their own marriage teetered too, or fell—we weren't certain which. It was early June, and after a teary, dramatic scene at the dinner table, my father moved to a bleak apartment complex on the far side of town. I never went there myself, but my sisters did, and reported back that it wasn't good—"depressing"—and consequently, my father still spent a lot of time around the house, mowing the lawn and fixing things and looking sad and confused, as if wondering how all this could have happened. How had it? He had a girlfriend, we had been gently informed, Willomena, the wife of a newer couple in town on the fringes of my parents' circle. I had a driver's license by then, and while driving aimlessly around town in my mother's Volvo I would sometimes go by her house, and there see my father's new used convertible—the metallic green Mustang—crouching in the driveway behind a bush that was the right color green, but not quite big enough to hide it entirely.

I had a job, along with several of my friends, as a groundskeeper at a local estate used for weddings and concerts and high school proms. The "castle," as it was called, was adjacent to the town beach, and there was a certain prestige that came with the job, second only to being a lifeguard. We got good tans, and spent our days cutting hedges and riding around on lawn mowers, and talking about the beautiful, inaccessible girls we would see on the beach on our days off—the pantheon of goddesses of our high school, tanned and bikinied, and taunting us with their beauty and friendliness and the knowledge that they had already entered the blessed kingdom of their own sexuality.

That summer several of my friends had decided they should earn certificates in "Junior Lifesaving," classes given by a childhood friend of my older sister, Sandra Jones, in the aqua blue swimming pool of her parents' backyard. Although she was not one of the preeminent beauties of her class, she was of the top social tier, and had a beautiful constellation of freckles that spread across her upper chest, just above the top of her floral bathing suit, and the pale, intoxicating edge of untanness, and it was she, more than any real interest in aquatic heroics, that was the motivating force behind our sudden interest in lifesaving. There was something vaguely romantic about the enterprise—the blue-green pool, the hot summer evenings, the grappling in the water with bathing-suited girls. I had no designs on Sandra, as she was clearly beyond my short romantic reach, but there were a couple of other, younger girls in the class: Laura Burns, the middle of the three Burns sisters, famous for their blond curly hair and ample breasts; and Laura's best friend, Julie Markos, the younger sister of one of my classmates, Jimmy, the smartest guy in my class. Julie had olive-colored skin, and frizzled brown hair, and a pretty round face with beautiful white teeth. I knew her from the previous winter, when we were taking the same gymnastics class at the junior high school, and I used to talk to her afterward in the sheltered, columned darkness of the school as we both waited to be picked up by our respective parents. She was a good athlete, we were told, could beat her brother in basketball and, it was rumored, wrestling. But she was two years younger than I, in my brother Charlie's class, and in the high code of adolescent morality, somehow off-limits. And although I had been told by Laura Burns that Julie "liked" me, and that I should call her, I was shy and inexperienced, was distracted by Sandra Jones, who had assumed an older-sisterly stance with me, and used me as a pet "victim" in lifesaving class—she demonstrated the "cross-chest carry," tugging me the length of the swimming pool with smooth, scissoring motions of her legs to the audience of my envious, guffawing peers.

My mother was not doing well that summer, vacillating among sorrow and sadness and rage. It was the summer when everyone was smoking, and during our Friday-night family dinners when my father came over, we would all sit around eating swordfish or lobster, and the soft summer sunlight would come slanting in through the porch windows, glinting through our wineglasses, and everyone would keep up an air of geniality until we got down to our third or fourth glass and the coffee and dessert, and then the cigarettes would come out—my mother first, and then my sister Lila, and then my younger brother, Charlie. Even I would bum one, and then my father, who had quit smoking fifteen years before, and dinner would end in one final conflagration of swirling smoke and bared emotions, angry words, tears, and the final, cathartic ritual of cleaning up—clearing and washing the plates, the clattering of plates and silverware, my father stepping meekly out of the back door and driving off, in voluntary exile.

Along with the news of their separation, we kids had somehow become privy to a lot of other, formerly classified information that I, for one, was not quite ready for: that my parents' marriage had already endured several cataclysms and traumas, other affairs and almost divorces and difficult entanglements with other people's husbands and wives. Both, as it turned out, had imperfect track records, and it had been my mother, surprisingly, who had strayed first, further muddying the waters. It had been the sixties, it was explained to us, and they had grown up in the sheltered and repressed fifties, and had married when they were in their early twenties—"babies," my mother said. Most of this had come through my mother, by way of my sisters, who interrogated her privately and then, happily, reported it to me. There had been a previous car crash, too, when I was about five or six—the time my mother drove the family station wagon through a stone wall on Route 1, leaving a few mowed-down trees and a gap in the wall, like a missing tooth, that I would study for years every time we drove by. My father had been having an affair at the time, we were told, and she had been on her way to her psychiatrist to discuss their possible separation and divorce, and had crashed the car partly "on purpose," as a form of protest. "I just lay down on the front seat and enjoyed it," she explained, and somehow her ploy had worked, and they stayed married.

But I was a sensitive child, finely attuned to their marital travails, and for a time I went to my own child's psychiatrist to work out my own troubles. I was "unhappy," my mother explained, and got lots of mysterious headaches that kept me out of school. After a year or two, I stopped, but it was this episode of childhood psychiatric care that Charlie seized upon and reminded me of whenever he got a chance.

"Oh," he would say happily, "that must have been when you were going to your psychiatrist!" He was two years my junior, and now, in his first year of high school, was not exactly thriving. He got mostly Cs on his report card, and had gotten in trouble for smoking, and dressed poorly, and seemed to be growing a potbelly. These and other imperfections I pointed out whenever I could, and his only chance at retribution was to remind me of my episode of mental unwellness. I got good grades in school, and was good in sports, and dressed with a great fussiness; my sister Lila was eighteen, and had taken up with Neil, a bearded, hippie type who drove a VW bus with faded flowers painted on the side. "He looks like Charles Manson, Mom," I would say when Lila was out of earshot. "He's ten years older than she is."

"Well, don't you worry about it. She seems very happy to us, and Neil has some very nice qualities."

"Like what?" I asked, but my mother had already checked out of the conversation. My youngest sister, Mary, was only thirteen, and largely escaped my keen eye. She was a bit overweight, was all, and I was fearful of her growing into a large, unpopular teenager. "Don't be silly," my mother would tell me. "And in any case, it's not your problem— we'll worry about your siblings; you just worry about yourself."

But what, I might have asked, was there to worry about? I was sixteen, and had already been accepted by a fancy prep school—my escape from the shifting emotional landscape of my family. And after the initial trauma of my parents' separation, I threw myself into a whirlwind of activities designed to prove to myself and my family that I was adjusting well to these difficulties, and was still on an upward-arcing trajectory of wholesome achievement.

Back at home my father came and went, my mother went back to her shrink; my older sister spent more and more time "out" with her bearded lover, and Charlie and Mary and I went about our business as best we could in our newly fatherless house. Our Friday-night dinner, *en famille*, continued as a ritual of transition, and generally went from cheerful to maudlin to sad, usually with some epiphany of anger or tears. One night at dinner, at about the time the cigarettes lit up, I made some clever remark at Charlie's expense, of the variety I had been making since his birth, almost fifteen years before, and without warning he leaped up from his falling chair and lunged toward me, and the next thing I knew I was on the floor, looking up at his scarlet face and, beyond, the startled spectators of my family. I did not retaliate, or even try to throw him off, realizing I had come up against some part of him that was better left alone. Besides, in not striking back, it occurred to me, in assuming a pacific stance, I could save some degree of face and dodge entire blame for the incident. It also occurred to me, down on the floor, that our days of hand-to-hand combat were over.

"Easy now, big boy," I said, staring up at him as he realized I had somehow tricked him again. He got up slowly, flustered and embarrassed, and tried to pull himself together. He lit up a cigarette, and then went out for a walk with my father to talk things over, and I tried to atone by helping to clear the table, but my mother took the opportunity to give me a little lecture.

"This whole thing is a lot harder on Charlie. He's going through a difficult time right now, so try to take it easy."

"And it's not difficult for the rest of us?"

"Well, of course it is, but you seem to be dealing with it better that Charlie and Lila. You have more going for you at the moment, if you don't mind my saying so."

"Like what?" I asked, calling her bluff.

"You know very well. And you don't need me to sing you your praises. We all know what they are, and we're very proud of you, but you have to be patient with the rest of us."

I could think of no adequate rejoinder, but could not help but think that it was *I* who had been tricked, now, scolded in the form of a compliment. And as I brought a load of dishes out to Lila—usually my ally—who was busy scrubbing the dishes, she took the opportunity to mutter, "Nice one, Mr. Perfect."

It was my turn at last. "Fuck you!" I said through clenched teeth, resisted the impulse to thump her on the back, and passing my father and Charlie on their way in, I went out for a walk of my own.

That was the familial rap on me—that I thought I was perfect, and everyone else in the world, or at least the family, was flawed. In truth, I worried a lot, and felt that my permissive parents were not adequately monitoring the behaviors of my siblings, and needed to be reminded periodically of their shortcomings. But they were tired of my telling them things they already knew, tired of the implication of their not being good parents. My mother was tired of my reminding her that smoking was not very good for her health. My father's only real shortcoming, as far as I could tell, was that he liked women too much, and I could not help but think that this was not a bad flaw to have.

Several weeks after the dinner-table incident my mother got back at me further when, after some clever remark of mine about Lila's boyfriend and her recent habit of not coming home at all at night—I was haunted by the image of her lying in some disheveled apartment with her pale, bearded lover—she coolly said, taking a slow drag on her cigarette, "Petey, let us worry about your brother and sisters. You don't have to be the family conscience anymore." I was sensitive as well as sharp-tongued, and I knew when I had been rebuked. Face burning, I silently left the room and went upstairs, resolved to spend more time away from all this, with my friends.

Julie Markos lived on the other side of the tracks that bent, in a long, silvery arc through the southern end of town. Hers was a pleasant street of the type developed in the fifties and sixties, straight and wide and smooth with handsome little houses that sat on quarter-acre plots of well-kept lawns—the kind of street we, who lived in older houses on the other side of town, snobbishly called "developments" and looked vaguely down on. It was not far from "Pole Alley"—a neighborhood inhabited by the descendants of Polish immigrants who had come here in the early part of the century to work in the town's single factory, which made lightbulbs, and not far from the Hellenic center, the site of summer Greek picnics, where my classmates reveled in their ethnic roots, playing tear-shaped guitars and expertly dancing to the exotic-sounding Mediterranean music that sifted up through the leaves of the overhanging elms. The Greeks and the Poles were the only intact ethnic groups in the town, and the ones we made jokes about, but the Greeks had gotten rich off the shellfish industry, and owned the town's two liquor stores. Julie's father—a slight, friendly man whom everybody liked—worked at the local elementary school in some janitorial capacity, and her brother was the class genius, the one we all gathered around in the free period before math class to "check" our homework.

The Greek picnics were an excellent opportunity for adolescent inebriation and romantic advances, and it was there that Laura Burns had told me about Julie Markos, that she "liked" me and was waiting for me to call. Laura even slipped me a small piece of paper with Julie's number scrawled on it in a smooth, loopy script. I had obeyed, and one summer evening arrived in front of her house in my parents' Volvo station wagon, and was halfway up the front walk when she emerged from the doorway, wearing white jeans and a blue sweater, her hair combed out from the middle in a way I had never seen before, revealing a luxuriant, kinetic energy. Through one of the windows of her house I could see her mother peering out at us as we got into the car and drove away. We went to a movie, I think, and drove around afterward, and ended up down in the beach parking lot, sitting in the warm, dark pocket of my car, talking. I was about to start the car and drive her home when she said, sounding disappointed, "Aren't you going to try to kiss me?" I looked over at her pretty round face, her eyes shining in the soft white glow of a single streetlight. I didn't have much confidence in my kissing, but I leaned toward her, and our lips met of their own accord. Her breath was warm and sweet, and her lips were full and soft, and as we kissed, my hand found a place to lie on the hard, strong curve of her back, and then crept around to the place where her ribs gave way to her belly, where it was met and held by her own, keeping guard. We paused now and then to catch our breath and look out across the lunar landscape of the parking lot before she finally said, "I'd better go." I started the car, but then she leaned toward me, and as we kissed again I watched her eyeballs roll upward against their half closed lids. The next time we paused for air, I pushed the shift into drive and drove her home.

Word travels fast among teenagers, and within a week or so, it was common knowledge among my friends that Julie and I were, for what it was worth, "going out." In life-saving class I took a certain private pride in her beauty, her smooth, brown belly, her strong legs and shoulders and arms, the swelling of her breasts. She was a better swimmer than I was, and stronger, and there was something vaguely alarming about being rescued by her, being held like a doll under her arm and pulled the length of the pool, her legs scissoring beneath me with powerful, muscular strokes. My own athletic prowess, as it turned out, did not translate to aquatic sports, and though I could swim well enough, I seemed to be less buoyant than even my male peers. This became a problem, I was to discover, when it came to saving a drowning person—holding him across the chest with one arm, and then pulling him, as my legs thrashed frantically beneath us, into shore. I had all the particulars under control, but when I headed off across the sloshing aqua pool, I could make little forward progress, and my head would go under between strokes, taking in mouthfuls of chlorinated water and gagging me, and I would have to give it up and save myself first. This aquatic failing was an embarrassment to me and a surprise to my friends and my instructor, who suggested I come in on the weekend for a special tutorial session. I even tried to save Julie, holding her smooth, porpoiselike body under my arm, but she was more amused than sympathetic, would not help, much, and left me to flounder and sink. But when we reversed roles and I became the "victim," she tucked me under her strong brown arm, and I could feel myself being pulled through the water like a rag doll and lay back and enjoyed it—water sloshing around my ears, the soft evening sky passing overhead, her strong, powerful legs working beneath me, saving me.

"See?" Laura said when we reached the far side of the pool. "It's easy, isn't it, Julie?"

"Kind of."

"Women float better than men," I protested. "It's scientifically proven—more body fat. I read about it in *National Geographic*."

"Yeah," said Greg Gates, a freckled, redheaded hockey player. "But you have more body fat between the ears." Laughter all around.

Once or twice a week I would borrow my mother's car and drive over to Julie's house, chat with her mother in their overly clean kitchen, and drive around for an hour or two in the summer twilight with her lovely fifteen-year-old daughter—down to the beach or the dump, along the narrow, wooded roads of our town. Although Julie was only fifteen, her mother sometimes let her drive the family car, and I, too, would sometimes let her drive around until dark, when we would stop and park. The car had a stick shift between the seats, which restrained my body's want to migrate over to hers and lie next to her, preferably with diminishing amounts of clothes. But Julie was no more eager to cross this boundary than I was, and was content with my rather desperate, inept kissing, my hand finding its way under her sweater to her smooth and olive-scented skin—belly and arms and ribs—toward, but never quite reaching, her breasts.

By day, my father and Charlie and I would drive over to the local nine-hole course to play golf—a summer ritual we had been partaking of for several years. We didn't talk much, just drifted around the course in pursuit of our errant shots, in admiration of our good ones; even Charlie and I suspended our traditional animosities while playing, and he, though generally erratic, was capable of bursts of semibrilliance. At sixteen, I had reached the point where I could occasionally beat my father, and though I took a certain pride in doing so, it also caused in me a certain ambivalence, suggesting, as it did, a turning point, a threshold—the point beyond which I would be getting better, and he worse. Finely attuned to the intersecting arcs of human existence—mine on the way up, his, I imagined, on the way down—I resisted indications that we all got older. But then the game would be over, we'd ante up our dimes and quarters, and my father would drop us off at the house and, without turning off the engine, continue around the circle and return to his new life. By this time he had given up his dismal apartment in town and moved into the city, where he'd be less tempted to come over and hang around, fixing things. But he still came to our Friday-night dinners, and a couple times he stayed for the weekend when my mother went away. That's when I got to drive around in the convertible with the roof down, sunk low in the seat, wheeling around corners, the wind in my hair—an American teenager on the prowl.

On one such beautiful midsummer's evening of low slanting sunlight and quavering leaves, I picked up Julie in front of her house and we headed north toward a tacky amusement park she had asked me to take her to. She looked pretty that night, tanner still, sunlight in her frazzled, combed-out hair. I had planned to stop on our way out of town for beer, but she brought from her oversized bag a bottle of Coke, and a smaller bottle of some clear, medicinal-looking liquid—"Rum and Cokes," she reported cheerfully. "You've never had them?"

"No, but there's a first time for everything." By the time we got there it was almost dark, and we were drunk: flashing, swirling lights, the smell of cotton candy, the din and clatter of rides and games, the shouts and laughter of giddy, intoxicated youth. Julie was clutching my arm by now, and we drifted through the crowds, played a game with little guns and corks, and came away, somehow, with an enormous stuffed panda bear, which she held under her other arm. Then we were up in the air, the three of us, suspended in a swaying metal box as the world swirled and tilted beneath us, and there were her lips again, and her pretty tan face, white teeth, and her warm, sweet breath, her hard, smooth body pressed against mine. And then my hand, in its drunkenness, found its way to her sweater, and then the shirt beneath it, and then to the silken softness of her bra, beneath which lay the sweet certainty of her breasts, which I briefly, miraculously held in my fumbling hand. Her breath was faster now, urgent, and as we swung, suspended, in the warm, summer air, I watched her eyes as they rolled upward against her half-closed lids, and our explorations were interrupted by one final jolt, the door of our cage swung open by a grizzly attendant, our panda spilling out and rolling onto the dusty, packed earth of the fairgrounds. We picked it up, and against Julie's protests, I led her slowly back through the crowds, through the sickening smell of popcorn and cotton candy, the braying come-ons of the game and ride people, and out into the darkness of the parking lot to our car, where we kissed some more, and in a moment of lucidity I managed to pour out the remaining contents of the rum and Coke, and left the bottles as evidence in the parking lot. Julie, it seemed to me, was drunker than I, but I was in no great shape either, and as we set off, the car seemed to sway and move in unexpected directions, and, conscious that we were in peril, I drove slowly, trying to peer through the haze of my own drunkenness. When we got to town I stopped in the high school parking lot while we devised a strategy for Julie to avoid her parents, but she was more interested in resuming our kiss, and I obliged. But a police car kept driving by, and I took her home, finally, walked her up to the front door, kissed her good-bye, and went home.

The next morning I was hungover, as was, I assume, Julie, because after that, her parents were somewhat cooler toward me. They had perhaps caught wind that my parents were separating, too, and therefore assumed I was in a volatile and unpredictable state, not to be trifled with. Little did they know it was Julie who was supplying the rum, and much of the passion, and that I, if anything, was a tempering force in our friendship.

It was about this time, midsummer, that I made my mother cry. I can't remember the particulars so much, except that it was one of our usual Friday-night dinners of flickering candlelight and too much wine, and we had reached the part of dinner of coffee and cigarettes and dessert, and the conversation had grown giddy and reckless—too many jokes, too fast—and my mother made some remark about how, if this kept up, and everyone kept leaving and going off to school, she was going to be the only one in the house that winter, and I added that the family dog, Jasper, would still be there to keep her company. The next thing I knew she was audibly weeping, head bowed to the table, tears dropping into her coffee and dessert and cigarette's smoke; Lila rushed to her side and hugged her as I looked on, mortified, knowing that in the court of my siblings, I would be held accountable. They went into the kitchen together, and my mother pulled herself together, and laughed it off as best she could, but her eyes were still red and swollen, and my father was trying to get away while the getting was good, and I, eager to escape the scene I had created, started to clear the table. This time, it was Charlie's turn to deliver the verdict I knew was coming. "Nice one, Mr. Perfect," he said bitterly. "You made Mom cry."

"Fuck you, fatso," I said, resorting to an outdated epithet of our childhood; Charlie wasn't really fat anymore, anyway, just big—one large troubled muscle absorbing beer and smoke. But he knew he had me, and softly repeated, as he left the room, "Nice one." A year before, I would have chased him into the other room and pummeled him into submission, but that was no longer an option. And besides, he was right. I *had* made her cry.

That weekend I got drunk again, at an impromptu party at the beach with lots of beer and glamorous, older girls, and a giant bonfire into which, late in the proceedings, I threw my only pair of sneakers: clouds of toxic black fumes rose up out of the flames; the rubber hissed and sputtered and finally melted like the wicked old witch in *The Wizard of Oz*. Julie wasn't there, but Sandra, my lifesaving teacher, was; she was sitting right beside me, in fact, and it was partly the erotic intoxication I got from bumping up against her and letting my arm slide down behind her back, and the glimpse of her breast in the flickering light of the fire, which caused me, in my feeble way, to try to impress her. I woke up the next morning both hungover and shoeless, and I had been rummaging around my closet for a couple of minutes before I recalled the scene of the night before—too much beer, and Sandra's warm body nearby, and the billowing smoke, my own hysterical, high-pitched laughter rising up over the flames. By the next day Julie had caught wind of my antics, adding to her growing suspicion that I was getting sort of strange.

It was true: it was August already, and it had become clear to me that I was never going to pull someone the entire length of a swimming pool; my parents were still separated, and it was growing less and less likely that the reunion they had described in June as "possible" was ever going to happen. Lila was still living with the bearded man with the Volkswagen, and had started, to my muffled horror, to talk of marriage. I tried to warn my mother but she shrugged it off, confirming my suspicion that I was out of the family loop—my stock was falling fast. They didn't know, apparently, that I was starting to get drunk and even had a girlfriend with whom I made out in distant amusement parks.

But I wasn't much of a boyfriend either, and I was beginning to disappoint Julie in small, accumulating ways. I had no sense of romance, for one thing, and didn't call her enough, didn't talk long enough when I did, and in a few short weeks I would be escaping to my fancy prep school and she would be returning to her dreary public high school, only a sophomore, three years to go. And perhaps she was disappointed I was not more adventurous than I was; I, too, was a virgin, and the world beyond loomed as a vast and murky swamp I had no particular desire to enter. "It's like," one of my more sophisticated friends informed me, "like a giant muscle has gotten ahold of you, and won't let go!" For me, Julie's lips were enough, her hair and the olive-toned skin of her belly, which, in a moment of recklessness, I had briefly kissed. But timidity, and the T-shaped stick shift of my father's car, thwarted my body's desire to merge with hers.

"Why don't you call her more?" Laura Burns would ask me while Julie was flopping around in the pool, saving someone.

"I do call her, at least once a week." Laura sighed heavily to indicate exasperation. She was wearing a flowered blue bathing-suit top, and I could see where the burnished brown of her tan ended in a pale blur. One of the advantages of having a girlfriend was that it brought you into a sort of filial intimacy with other, previously inaccessible girls, who gathered around as coaches and confidantes.

"She doesn't think so," Laura reported. "Not very often, anyway." In truth, though, I was still pretty wrapped up with my friends, working by day, playing sports in the evening—running and kicking and scoring goals, trying to reassert my place in the pecking order, atone for my lifesaving shortcomings.

By this time, Julie had begun to sulk, and describe me as "weird," a suspicion that was confirmed one evening after I picked her up, and we drove out to the golf course and parked on the road beside the eighth hole, and I asked her to walk out onto the green with me. Then I asked her to touch it with her hand—its wonderful, impossible smoothness—and then suggested that we lie down there, together. For a couple of years now I had been haunted by the vision of a naked woman lying on a golf green, under a dome of flickering stars, with me hovering nearby, then lying down beside her. She laughed nervously, and refused, and stood on the fringe of the green. I tried to persuade her, but she then wondered if I was "perverted, or something." I gave up and got sullenly back into the car, but as I drove her the long, slow way home, she kept looking over at me and laughing nervously. "You're kind of weird." It was a relief, finally, to reach her orderly, tree-lined street and drop her off. In revenge, I didn't even walk her up to the front door. Then I drove through town a couple times, listening to the radio, and went home.

My father's car was in the driveway, and my parents were inside on the couch, talking. I got a whiff of the solemnity of the occasion, and hung around long enough for them to see that I was sober, and then snuck upstairs to bed, closed the door, and took refuge in a pile of back issues of *National Geographic*. I must have fallen asleep in the middle of a long, photo essay on sheep shearing in Australia, because the next thing I heard was my father's car starting up outside, and then crunching around the driveway and accelerating away into the night, and as I opened my eyes, my mother was there, walking into my room, wiping her eyes, and then she was sort of falling toward me, collapsing onto the bed and into my arms that had reached up to catch her. "Oh, Petey," I heard her say, between sobs. "I love you so much." And then she was in my arms, her large woman's body pressed against mine, weeping. "I'm so frightened of being left alone," she said, and I felt like I was about to start crying too.

"Oh, Mom," I heard myself saying, and then we were just lying there, rocking slowly back and forth on the bed. And she slowly pulled herself together, sat up, and wiped her bloodshot eyes. "I guess I've had better summers," she said, laughed, and tucked me into bed, and went back to being my mother. I returned to my article on sheep, but as I fell asleep, finally, I was haunted by the remembered weight of her body, its large, maternal shape, at once strange and mysterious and familiar, pressed against mine.

After that, things started to happen quickly. On the evening of my final lifesaving test, I quietly arranged to do something else, by way of excuse, and called Sandra Jones when she was at work, and left a message with her mother that I couldn't make it to the lifesaving test that night, and would call again to arrange a makeup. But when? Summer was slipping away.

A week or so later I picked up Julie in front of her house, for what turned out to be our final date. A reddish late-summer sun was slanting down through the tired-looking leaves, and I was driving the Mustang that night, as my mother had gone away for the weekend, and my father was looking after us. Julie was sullen, and quiet, and I suspected she was gearing up to break up with me. When I tried to get something out of her she would say it was "nothing," and look down and away, through the window. She was pretty when sad, her wavy brown hair parted in the middle, and she was wearing a white cashmere sweater that made her skin, after a summer on the beach, look even a deeper, darker brown. We drove in silence down Fletcher Road, and we were about to turn down Juniper Lane when I impulsively pulled over and asked if she wanted to drive—a last-ditch attempt to cheer her up and postpone my return to teenage bachelorhood. It worked, too, at first, and Julie looked cute in the driver's seat, peering up over the wheel, and seemed to be getting happier, and at one point I laid my hand on her knee as we rolled along the narrow country road, stripes of sunlight flashing through the trees.

"What's on the radio?" she asked. I reached down to find something on the dial, and she reached down to help me and must have forgotten that she was driving, because when I next looked up the car had just started angling into the woods—mowing down those little white cement guardrails, chunks of cement bouncing up over the car, and once we were finished with those we started in on the trees—clunk, clunk, clunk, clunk, clunk—until we met one big enough to put a stop to the macabre charade, and left us, a washed-up teenage couple, sitting in a car in the woods, the crumpled hood hissing out steam and smoke, the radio faithfully playing the final, staticky ballad of our summer romance.

The rest, needless to say, was a bit of a blur—out of the car, quickly, and up onto the deserted road, following Julie as she paced around in small, tightening circles, mumbling to herself, "Oh my God. Oh my God. I don't believe it. Oh my God." But then, before the police and tow trucks came, I captured her long enough in my arms to tell her the plan that had come to me even as we were still plowing through trees: that it was I, and not she, who had been driving. She was only fifteen, after all, didn't even have a license, and the only way to get the insurance money and avoid a fuss and a scandal was for me to take the blame. She was unconsoled, and kept pacing around in tiny circles, but when the flashing lights and soft-spoken men arrived and pulled the car out of the woods, I told them that we had both been looking for a station on the radio, and the next time I looked we were driving into the woods. I left out the part about Julie being at the wheel.

We got a ride into town, and in the shadow of an enormous maple tree up the street from her house, I tried to console her further, told her it would be all right and not to worry, but she had been rendered wordless by the crash, and sullen, and I could not help thinking how pretty she looked in the soft glow of the street. "Go to bed," I finally suggested. "I'll call you tomorrow." And then I watched her go up the walk to the house. I ran into town and called my father from a phone booth, so he would have time to get used to the idea before I got home. He, too, sounded shocked, and tired, and by the time I had run, and walked, and talked my way the final mile home, he was in something of a state, pacing around and blaming himself for trusting his kids so much with the cars. In the web of his ramblings, it sounded like he was blaming his own marital troubles for the crash. "Nonsense, Dad. I just fucked up. We were fiddling with the radio, and the next time I looked we were driving into the woods. We weren't even drinking beers. I can pay for it, anyway. I've been working all summer."

"Well, I'm sure the insurance will cover it," he said with a resigned sigh. "We can talk in the morning. But you're sure you're not hurt, right? No headaches or anything? Whiplash? You feel all right?"

"Yeah, I'm fine. We weren't even going very fast."

"But you think the car's totaled?"

"I think so. That's what the tow truck guy said."

"Huh."

He was still in a daze, I could tell, pacing around the room, and then went back to blaming himself. "Maybe we were too liberal with you kids and the cars. . . . It's been a long hard summer for all of us. Well, no use moping. . . . Why don't you go up to bed? We can talk in the morning."

"Okay, Dad. Sorry about all this. Shit."

In the morning, news of my calamity had preceded me to work, and my friends were having a field day speculating on the causes of the crash—I was practicing the cross-chest carry; Julie was giving me a blow job while driving; etc., etc. I bore it all as my due but was relieved when, after lunch, they gave it up and moved on to other things. By the time I got home that afternoon, my father had already been up to visit his old car and taken a few Polaroids of its crumpled front end which he kept trying to show me, but I couldn't bear to look. He had already been to the insurance company and been assured they would be able to cover it—I was insured, after all—and he assumed a detached, sardonic attitude toward the whole mishap. "Maybe it's time I gave up with convertibles anyway," he said. "All that sunlight can't be good for you, can it? They're starting to come out with studies about it, you know. Plus, they're dangerous—they throw you out through the roof. That's the third—maybe that's enough. We're lucky one of us wasn't really hurt. You're sure you're all right, now? That car is pretty well smashed up!"

My siblings, too, were amused by my crash, as it seemed to indicate I was not as perfect as they thought I thought I was. I absorbed it all, protected by the invisible shield of the truth—the private knowledge that I hadn't been driving, anyway, that my automotive slate was still clean.

My mother wasn't angry either. "Serves him right," she said happily, meaning my father. "I never did like that car anyway. Acting like a playboy, sneaking around town to see his mistress." She confessed that she, too, used to drive up past Willomena's house, and would see the car up in the back, crouching in the shadows. "In any case," she added jauntily, "if he wants a new wife, let him have a new car, too—out with the old, in with the new." Lately, she had received some attentions from some of the men in the town—the unremarried halves of divorced couples—and was regaining some of her buoyancy.

And within a couple of days my father did have a new car—a dull, used brown Maverick, bought from a friendly car dealer who sometimes played in his poker group. While I tried to put the whole episode out of my mind, in my past, I did feel a twinge of regret at the sight of my father behind the wheel of the brown, hard-roofed car. My accident had brought the age of convertibles to a close.

The summer, too, was winding down. I kept procrastinating, not calling Sandra to reschedule my lifesaving test, which my friends, including Julie, had already passed. "It was simple," they kept telling me, and I knew it was—for people who float. I was a "sinker," Sandra had already informed me, and this, I knew, would never change. I had already adjusted to the notion that saving someone's life after a shipwreck was something I'd never do—I'd have to just throw a lifesaving ring. I tried not to dwell on my failings, and instead looked forward to the fall, and escaping to my fancy prep school. I went downtown and bought some new clothes, I went for long, intense training runs to get in shape for the season, and I silently worried about what it would be like in the big house without me to protect my mother and younger siblings from intruders. Against my muffled protests Lila moved in with the bearded lover, Neil, and only returned now and then to show us how grown up she was and get a change of clothes.

As for Julie, the car accident had served as a kind of emphatic punctuation to our relationship—not a period, exactly, but something stronger than a comma. I had called her once to tell her that everything was all right, that my father already had a new car, but I had gotten her mother instead, who seemed to have cooled further. It was several days before Julie called me back, but she sounded sullen and sheepish. I couldn't pick her up anymore, because I didn't want to ask for the use of the car, but I would see her at the final dance of the summer, held at the Hellenic Center, not far from her house.

It was, as you might expect, a melancholy affair—a dimly lit room, a crowd of apprehensive teenagers, the succession of that summer's favorite songs being played by a mediocre but heartfelt band of long-haired pretenders. They were good at the slow, schmaltzy ones, like "Stairway to Heaven," and the established lovers stepped forward and swayed around in small, intimate circles, but not Julie and I. She was late, for one thing, and when she finally arrived she was surrounded by an entourage of protective girlfriends, hovering like bodyguards. But they all got up to dance, finally, and I drifted over through the shadows and stood beside her. Then we danced a couple of times, and I held her lightly as we swayed around, the familiar curve of her back in my hands, taking in the scents of cashmere, shampoo, and the other fragrances that hover around fifteen-year-old girls and fill the bedrooms where they spend their solitary nights. I asked her if she wanted to go outside for a minute to talk, she nodded, and we wandered across the dance floor and went outside to see if I could lull her back to life. The dim light of a half-moon fell across the parked cars, and the air was filled with the rasp of crickets, and I came up behind her and held her in my arms, buried my face in her frazzled hair. I asked her what was the matter, and told her my parents had already forgiven me. She turned around, and I studied her sad, sweet, downcast face, soft and lunar in the moonlight. I hugged her, and tried to kiss her, but her lips were passionless and dry, and there was no longer that supple, yielding quality to her body, laden with possibility. I didn't know if it was the car, or me, or the fact that in a few days, I would be leaving for school, and when I asked her, all I got was a barely audible "Everything." I held her hand, and as I led her back through the cars, past the shadows of murmuring couples, it was clear that we were no longer among them, that the low, innocent trajectory of our summer love was on its final descent and, like a shooting star, was burning out in midair.

"I'll see you before I go back to school," I said feebly at the doorway, but even then it had the ring of an untruth, and back inside, we were both reabsorbed into the clusters of our friends. By the time my friends and I left the dance, the long-haired musicians had been replaced by some clean-cut Greek kids who, to our amazement, started playing their twangy, hard-on-the-ears music, and the last I saw of Julie she was just one pretty, smiling face in a big, hand-holding circle of her friends, expertly circling the floor in a series of intricate and effortless steps—two forward, one back, two forward, one back—and before I knew it I was sitting in the back of someone's Volkswagen Bug with a couple of my friends and a six-pack of beer, my sadness subsumed by the cloud of blue smoke that filled the car—the "summer harvest" of the marijuana that had grown in their parents' backyard.

A week later, my family held a farewell dinner of sorts for me, lobster and candlelight and evening sunlight, slanting with an autumnal tint into the room. My dad was there, as he'd always been, and Neil had broken into the inner circle of the family, somehow, and he sat in silence, mostly, watching, and gently kneading his beard—like a visiting archaeologist quietly examining the shifting bones of the family. We gave him a good show that night: the old geniality back, wine flowing, jokes flying, my parents, at opposite ends of the table, looking much as they always had—in my eyes, still the perfect couple. I was proud of them, somehow—proud that even though they were at odds, they could still sit down and have a peaceable dinner with their overgrown children, just like old times. And although it was clear by this time that they were never going to get back together, it also occurred to me that night that our family was still intact, somehow, and that whatever was going to happen, we were all in it, more or less, together.

Earlier that day on the golf course my father had told me he was proud of how well I was doing, and was sorry that their marital difficulties had come just as I was getting ready to go off to school, and he hoped it all didn't affect my ongoing, unspoken program for self-improvement. I tried to assure him that it wouldn't and, as if in proof, played well that day.

"You should have seen him on the course," he reported at dinner. "He almost beat me, the little rat."

"He's so competitive," Lila said, in such a way to indicate that she didn't consider competitiveness a virtue. Through his beard, Neil managed a little smile.

"Now all he has to do," Charlie chimed in, "is learn how to drive."

The barb was too crude for a rejoinder, and, if nothing else, I had learned that summer the subtle power of silence.

"Yeah, Pete," Charlie continued, not content with my lack of response. "Are you going to go out with Julie again, or won't her parents let her drive with you anymore after you drove her into the woods?"

This was beginning to irk me, but I held my tongue. Charlie was bigger than I now, and harboring fifteen years of pent-up fraternal animosities. But if he had had a crystal ball there at the dinner table, instead of an oft replenished glass of wine, he would have seen that two family vehicles awaited their destruction at his own hand, on the same bend of road within a half mile of our house—one going into town, the other coming home—both with high levels of alcohol and adolescent confusion coursing through his veins. He still had a hard row to hoe, and it would be he, and Mary, and my mother who would bear the brunt of the new family order—spending the winter in the cool and fatherless house.

This was the first public mention of my friendship with Julie Markos, and my mother played dumb. "What, who?" she was saying, with a little smile, pretending she knew nothing, but the sound of Julie's name had caused me to turn inward, like a man in a trance, gazing into the yellow light of the candles, and as the banter of my family went happily on without me, it slowly dawned on me that it was I who had failed her, though I wasn't certain how, or why: our imperfect love was spawned at the edge of a swimming pool, under a canopy of summer leaves. Her belly was smooth and brown, like a child's, her lips full and sweet, tasting faintly of coconut. Her hair was frazzled and silken, and her sweatered breasts were not large, but wonderfully present, the color of moonlight, and were willing to be held in my fumbling, adolescent hands. I loved her as best I could, which wasn't, as it turned out, very well. One summer night, in the twilight of our love, I let her drive my father's car, and together we rode it into the woods, and thereby brought the age of convertibles to a close.

It would be years before, at this same table, I revealed to all my secret—played the final trump card of my youth—but until then it was mine to keep, like a precious jewel—a private cloak of martyrdom. I had Julie's honor and reputation to protect, after all, and it was the least I could do by way of gratitude, for among the many gifts she had given me that summer, her love among them, she had inadvertently relieved me of the tiresome burden I had been carrying around with me since childhood: after she crashed my father's car, no one called me "Mr. Perfect" anymore, and I quietly became, in a way that I had never been, just one of the family.

The Woman from Out of Town

On these Tuesday afternoons of his lessons, William was overcome by a certain heaviness, a gathering apprehension which, as his eyes distractedly fell on the flaxen hair of Debbie Somers, not two feet away, manifested itself as a slowing down of time. Above him, the slow hands of a pale clock worked their way around on the final revolution of the school day, and from his seat he could hear the faint growl of its turning—the unseen meshing of countless tiny gears. But his eyes lay on her hair, the perfect curve of her shoulder, the irregular pattern of freckles on the nape of her neck like an undiscovered constellation of stars. He would have liked to reach out and touch them, connect them to each other like the drawings in children's magazines. But even her lovely half-turned face, her flushed and freckled cheek, the pout of her pretty lips, only compounded his sense of subdued dread, and brought home with heightened clarity the fact that, two hours hence, he would be sitting in a quiet, dimly lit room before the enormous black mass of the piano, under the disappointed gaze of his instructor—a sallow young man nervously kneading a wispy yellow beard.

"And if we have this problem tomorrow," his teacher was saying in her thin dead voice, pacing around before them like a caged animal, "I guarantee you will *all* have to stay after school—a minute for every time I have to raise my voice." The class was lulled to silence less by shame than by a collective apprehension that they were about to see their teacher cry; yet her ruse, William noticed, had never worked, for after the first few marks on the board—a minute after school for each—the students were overcome by a kind of giddy indifference, and as her small, round face grew red and hot, she realized they had called her bluff, the din slowly rose, and order swiftly dissolved.

And something in the way Debbie's hair lay on her collar, or the way her purple sweater was pulled off center, revealing to him the confluence of her shoulder, neck, and back—the place where they all miraculously converged—induced in him a memory of the night before: as he lay in bed trying to sleep, he had heard his parents talking—his mother teasing his father about something, and his father weakly defending himself, staving off her gibes with laughter which, while deflecting her charges, seemed to half admit their truth. They were speaking softly, in tones with which he was not familiar, and he could not make out clearly what was being said—only that it was about his father; he could picture them, lying together in the bed, and he wanted to speak out and tell them to be quiet, but instead he wrapped his head in his pillow, listened to the rhythms of his own breathing and, in time, fell asleep.

The final words of the teacher's harangue were blotted out by the ringing bell, and William moved quickly, gathered his books, and went out, out past Debbie Somers and through the subtle fragrance that hovered around her, down the hall, and, beating the throng to the door, through it and out—running now across the tired grass of the school yard, down the hill and over the bridge to the road that wound the remaining mile to his house. There he slowed to catch his breath and then ran again, to the next telephone pole, walked to the next, then ran and so on until he reached his yard, ran across it and in through the back door and into the heavy stillness that filled the house on weekday afternoons: a cat lay sleeping in a sunlit chair, a fly buzzed around a bowl of fruit, a note lay on the kitchen table: "Will— Dad will pick you up a little after three to take you to your lesson. See you at suppertime. XOXOXO Ma." And then he remembered something else, that today the routine was somewhat different: his mother was in the city, seeing her psychiatrist, and his father was being interviewed by someone—a woman from some foreign country, he dimly remembered—and his father had to drop her off at the train station after his lesson. This complication came as an irritant and further darkened his mood, for even in the weekly torpor of his lessons William took a certain solace in routine, the predictable cycle of dread and redemption, of the heaviness which turned in the course of an hour to an almost unbearable lightness and sense of well-being as he and his father drove home together through the last lingering light of day. But the woman and the train changed all this, tipped toward despondency the delicate balance of external events and internal moods in which he lived.

His mother and father were young, and while growing up he had always taken an unspoken pride in their beauty, a kind of spontaneous vitality he did not find in other children's parents. When he and his siblings played kickball in the backyard on warm summer nights, his father often joined them, stroking the soft red ball over the back fence and then wheeling around the bases on his long, loose legs; and at an early age he had become conscious of his mother's beauty—a beauty both of the loving, maternal kind and of something else—a woman in a black bathing suit with a broad, tan back, strolling down the beach in the soft, pinkish light of early morning, bending to pick up a shell, or chasing after one of her four children and carrying him, shrieking, into the sea. Even her footprints seemed to him deep and mysterious and lovely—the deep smooth valley of her heel, the high swell of her arch, the discrete impressions of each perfect toe. In comparison, he noticed, his own footprints were blurry and insubstantial, easily erased by a single wave lapping onto the sandy shore.

His parents led an active social life too—volleyball and tennis on weekends, dinners and cocktail parties which he would sometimes hear as he lay in bed, the tingling of forks and knives and glasses, the smell of smoke, sudden bursts of laughter and the endless din of conversation which later turned to the sad, sweet laments of music and the sounds of shuffling feet as they danced. And William knew—for he had once looked down through the rungs of the banister onto this strange, mysterious sight, a roomful of grown-ups, holding each other and swaying around the room—that his parents did not only dance with each other.

In the summers his father drove with the roof of the convertible down and sometimes played the radio—lilting love songs sung, William had always imagined, by beautiful brown-skinned women in far-off cities. And these songs, William could see, moved his father, filled him with thoughts and feelings of other places and people he had never seen.

William was outside when his father arrived, his blue Fairlane veering into the driveway, sending a flock of starlings leaping up into the air from the branches of the enormous elm tree with a sudden, airy rush: he imagined he could feel the winds generated by their thousands of flapping wings.

The car came to a stop with a slight skid and William climbed in.

"Good afternoon," his father said cheerfully. "Sorry I'm a little late—do you have everything, all your music?"

"Yes," William said, his father pushed the car into drive, and with a little lurch they spun around the driveway and out into the road. His father's legs were long and, as he drove, folded downward, like wings. He wore a pair of old, faded sneakers, flecked with paint, and on each shoe a small slit had been made with a razor blade, relieving pressure on his little toes.

"How was school?" his father asked; William could feel him looking over at him.

"Good," William said, but could not summon more of an answer. "You have to pick someone up after my lesson?"

"Oh, yes. Thanks for reminding me—a Miss Delgado. She came to interview me for some reason, and I've got to pick her up while you're in your lesson. Then we can drop her off in Harrington on the way home. I'm sorry about all this, but it's the only way we could think of doing it."

"That's all right," William said, but privately wondered why she had not been picked up earlier and taken to the train then. He thought of his father's studio, a large, airy room smelling of paint and turpentine and smoke where his father spent his days, painting and drawing and talking on the phone to people in far-off cities. It must have been there that he was interviewed, on the old vinyl couch that sat, mainly unused, along one wall. Then he thought of his mother, driving in to see her psychiatrist—a short, balding man who greeted William, when they once met, with what seemed unwarranted familiarity.

Outside, the landscape moved past with a rising sense of the inevitable—an aging barn in a field, two horses by a fence, the liquor store where they sometimes stopped on the way home, and then the church where he would have his lesson.

"Do you want me to come in?" his father asked.

"I'll be fine," William said.

"You sure? I'll be back in half an hour then. Have a good lesson—it will be great." He smiled and raised a clenched fist of encouragement. He would usually come in and sit in the warm, homey lobby, a book resting on his folded knee.

"Okay," William said, and trudged up the stairs and in. But the secretary, Mrs. Morgan, was not at her desk, and all was unusually quiet. On the wall was a large, pale clock— an exact duplicate of the one in William's classroom, except that it moved not with the slow, imperceptible motion of the tides, but with a sudden, emphatic burst of energy whereby the minute hand leaped from one minute to the next, as it did now, from 3:28 to 3:29. Like a man walking to the gallows, William trudged up the hall to his room, where, to his surprise, the door was open and no one was inside. Even the lid of the piano was closed like a coffin. William sat down anyway, suppressing his hopes, and looked out onto the parking lot, across which moved the pink shadow of a cloud. He heard footsteps, the squeak of a door, and felt his face flush with disappointment, his hopes dashed—until he saw that it was not his teacher but rather a smiling Mrs. Morgan who appeared in her pink cat's-eye glasses, her hands collapsing by her sides in mock exasperation.

"There you are!" she said. "I've been trying to reach you for the last half hour. Mr. Fitzpatrick had to leave during his last lesson—it seems his wife is having a baby—at least they think so. Is your father still here?"

"No. But he'll be back. It's only half an hour."

"Oh, isn't that a shame! Well, you can use the room to practice, or you can come down to the office—we have some nice books in there you might want to read. So sorry!" She taped a note to the door and disappeared, and then William fled too, but in the other direction, listening to the faint cacophony of sounds—a halting flute, a squeaky violin, a

tentative piano—that leaked out from behind closed doors:
an unrehearsed orchestra for mediocre child musicians. He
drifted to the end of the hall where two wooden doors were
opened onto the church—a vast, dimly lit space filled with a
soft yellow light, the distant altar framed by a high stained-
glass window in whose jagged, luminous shapes William could
make out the figure of a man, hanging by his hands from a
cross. He stood for a moment, looking, and after what seemed
a respectful pause went outside.

Low, puffy clouds floated overhead, and a few dry leaves
scuttled across the parking lot in the wind. He knocked a
stone loose from the dirt and kicked it across the parking lot
to a split-rail fence on the edge of the field. His new lightness of mood was dampened somewhat by the thought of
the woman and the train, and he wondered where his father
was now: picking her up at the Agawam Motel—a low,
skulking place with a shallow, greenish pool, driving back
with her to pick him up from his lesson that never happened. He imagined her as younger than his mother—the
kind of woman his father could make laugh, and for whom,
on the volleyball court, he would shed his shirt and dive in
the dust for balls other fathers would lamely grope for, as if
bending down to pet a cat, the ball bouncing off their shins
and, as they apologetically groaned, rolling into the tall
grass. At net his father would leap high and, with long, re-
volving arms, thump the ball down onto opposing players'
heads, women fleeing in mock terror and then ducking under the net to scold him for playing "too hard," hitting him
with feigned, halfhearted punches.

William, too, fancied himself a keen judge of beauty
and, at age eleven, had already assembled a private pantheon
of women he considered worthy of his admiration—Debbie
Somers; Mrs. Thomas, his third-grade teacher; Annie Mey-
ers, his older sister's best friend, whom he would sometimes
follow—the long, swaying rope of her hair—on the way to

school. He had once asked his father if he thought Samuel Woolf's mother was beautiful, but felt confused and rebuffed by his answer: "I think all women are beautiful."

As William walked back across the parking lot he could see, among the cars that passed on the road, his father's blue Fairlane. He ran inside to retrieve his music, and by the time he returned, the car was waiting by the front door. In the passenger's seat sat a woman with frizzy brown hair, streaked with gray, smiling oddly at him.

"You must be William," she said, opening the door and holding out a long, slender hand with a large gold ring. "I'll get in back," she said, but before she had moved, William had slid into the seat behind her.

"Oh, thank you. I'm Miriam."

"That's almost William, isn't it?" his father said. "Upside down, or backward?" The woman laughed, and they drove out of the parking lot and onto the road.

"How was your lesson, Will?"

"Canceled," William said, taking a certain pleasure in the word.

"Canceled?" his father asked, incredulous, turning to him.

"Yeah—Mr. Fitzpatrick's wife is having a baby, I think."

"Is she really? And you've been waiting all this time? What did you do?"

"Walked around in the field. I saw a hawk."

"Well, I *am* sorry," his father said. "This *has* been a day of complications."

"It's really all my fault," the woman said, turning sideways in her seat. "What grade are you in, William?"

"Fifth."

She did not respond but studied him for a moment with soft greenish eyes in which, William thought, he could make out faint, iridescent flecks of blue.

"He looks just like you," she now observed to William's father, and turned her mysterious gaze to him.

"Do you think so?" His father said. "That's nice to know."

The woman spoke with a faint accent of some other place, and as she looked at his father William watched her—the faint, etched lines radiating outward from the corners of her eyes, and the look on her face, neither young nor old, that somehow suggested she had never had children of her own.

"But I am sorry about the inconvenience. It's really all my fault," she repeated unnecessarily, "not your father's."

By the time they reached the station it was almost dark. They piled out of the car, and from the trunk William's father took her suitcase, a small, strange, boxlike thing, and set it down on the platform. As they waited, William drifted away toward the farther end of the platform, looking vaguely out over the empty parking lot toward the light of a neon sign that said "Rexall Drugs" in long, wavering script. In the west, over the peaked roofs and church spires of the town, streaks of red and pale blue stretched across the horizon, and from somewhere arose the plaintive sound of a dog's bark, and for an instant, there was a delicious sensation of suspension, of standing still—day turning to night, summer to fall—like that instant before the second hand of the clock leaped from one minute to the next. And from somewhere else came the sound of bells.

When he turned he could see that they, too, had moved a few steps away, the suitcase abandoned on the platform, and now stood with not much space between them—his father straight and tall in the half light, the woman, shorter, looking up at him and saying something William could not hear; but he could sense its gentle weight, and hear the soft, tingly sound of her laughter that drifted down the steel rails and made him wish, suddenly, that the train would come and take her away. He walked farther and tried to hear nothing and would have blocked his ears with his thumbs had they not been there to see him; when he looked again they were still standing there, like two magnets of the same pole, wanting to be closer but held apart by some invisible, mysterious force: and *he*, William then realized, was that force, the part of the equation that did not fit, and it was his stumbling, shuffling presence at the end of the platform that kept them apart, kept them from succumbing to whatever it was they both felt. For an instant, he hated both himself and them for putting him there.

He peered down the track but there was nothing, only the glint of the rails converging in the distance and disappearing around the bend. He kicked a rock along the platform, glanced again at the woman and his father and then back down the tracks where a single red light had finally appeared, shimmering closer; and then there was the sound of bells, like Christmas, the flashing of lights, and all was suddenly animate, alive again, like the set of a play come to life—William drifting back up the platform, his father and the woman strolling back, and all three silently converging at the suitcase, and then the enormous, lumbering train, creaking and rocking toward them like some sort of tired prehistoric beast.

"Well, it was nice to meet you, William," the woman said, reaching out to shake his hand and beaming down at him with what seemed excessive friendliness—the hopeful fondness of women who liked his father. Her hand was soft and cool and faintly damp.

She picked up her strange squarish suitcase, the conductor hopped off the hissing train, and William turned back toward the car, uneager to witness this final moment of parting, but out of the corner of his eye he sensed his father bending to receive a kiss, a final murmured word, a touch of the hand, an affectionate glance at William, and then she was gone, and the train rocked away through a veil of its own steam like a scene from some old late-night movie.

"Well!" his father said, and together they turned and walked back to the car in silence, the doors closing like clapped hands, the car starting up and easing out of the parking lot and onto the road and out of town. As he sat, William could picture the woman on the train, settling into her seat, gazing out the window onto an unfamiliar landscape of school yards and houses and passing lights.

"What was her name again?" he asked, less out of a desire to know than to fill the silence.

"Ah, Del-ga-do," his father said, deliberately, a new lightness in his voice, as if he, too, was relieved. "An Italian from Montreal, I guess. I don't even know how I get into these things—you accept a month in advance as if it would never happen, and then it does and you have to go through with it anyway. Are you missing any good TV shows?"

"Not really."

Again, the silence settled between them, but William wanted to keep talking, did not want to give his father a chance to think—about the woman, or about him, or that he blamed him for liking her.

"I guess my teacher has a baby now."

"Yes! Isn't that nice," his father said. "And wasn't it nice of the baby to be born on the day of your lesson. You'll have to get him a little present, won't you—a little rattle, maybe?"

William laughed, and briefly imagined that this baby would prevent his teacher from coming next week, and the week after, and thereby end his musical career forever.

"Yes, isn't that nice," his father repeated softly, and then braked and veered quickly onto the dirt parking lot of Harrington Liquors.

"Wine," he said. "I think your mother wanted us to stop and get some wine—white, I think. Do you want anything? Salted nuts, a bag of pretzels, maybe?"

"No thanks," William said, knowing that his father would get him something anyway.

"Do you want to come in? I'll only be a second."

"That's all right," William said, not wanting to dislodge the sense of well-being which, since they had left the train station, had slowly returned to him. "I'll wait here."

He watched his father take three long strides across the liquor store parking lot and then disappear inside. He sat for a moment and then reached out and turned on the radio, and there it was—one of those sad, sweet love songs, sung by a wistful, beautiful woman in some distant city, her voice rising and falling through the static hiss that now filled the car, like snow. He tuned it in as best he could, and then kept his finger on the dial, as if to improve the reception, somehow, absorb the sadness and beauty of the song and hold it in the cool dark pocket of the car, like a precious gift, for his father.

Shining So Nicely
in the Sun

When I first got the car it still smelled of the farm—the sweet, musty scents of hay and animals and people that filled the house and barn, that my grandmother has carried around in her hair and clothes—the layered, animal fragrances that came with living in the same stone house for most of her eighty-four years. She has had a dog, always, and a horse named Talbot, long since dead, and a fluctuating population of cats who lived in the barn and woods and in an old smokehouse beside the back door. Cats were everywhere—on the roof of the car and under bushes and in the stable of the barn, and moved around the place with a spooky, liquid motion, padding little paths of transit across the lawn with their soft, relentless paws. Birds, too, flocked to the feeders she had hung outside her windows, and to the dead trees she let stand on the edge of the woods so they would have a place to live. And it was no coincidence that her car was named after a bird, too, Skylark, and enjoyed a kind of honorary place in the animal kingdom, and sat crouching by the back door on the ruts it had worn for itself on the grass.

The last time I went to visit her it was late summer, or early fall—the second weekend of September. When I got off the bus the car was not there, waiting by the curb as it always was, and in its absence the city seemed hostile, unfriendly. She had told me she would send for a cab, that it would be waiting when I arrived, but several buses had come at once and there was a line of people waiting. My several attempts to call a taxi of my own were unsuccessful, and it was half an hour before everyone had been picked up and taken off, and I was able to get someone to drive me out to the farm.

The driver is a thin, heavy-smoking man with a thick Bucks County accent, and he doesn't know where Joanna is. I point him out Route 10, but we run into evening traffic and it is twenty minutes before we clear the city limits, cross over the bridge on the outskirts of Reading and roll along past the unused factories and deserted train yards, past the condominium complexes and golf courses and newly built industrial parks that have sprouted up where fields had once been. But then we rise up past the sandstone church, past the graveyard on the hill where my grandfather is buried, past the softball field where, on summer evenings, plump, pretty Pennsylvania girls play in the twilight, shouting and laughing amid the swirling sparks of fireflies. We turn left down Weaver Road and roll along between the fields of corn and fruit trees, and then onto the familiar dirt road and onto the grass in front of the barn. I pay the man and escape his bluish cloud of smoke, and as I cross the lawn I see my grandmother's face in the window, looking out. She meets me at the door; I kiss her on the cheek and step into the sweet, moldering fragrance of the house.

"You made it!" she says. She has grown thinner since I last saw her, smaller—something she had never been able to do when she was in better health. She has lost her appetite, and does not have much energy for cooking, and now that she no longer drives, she doesn't even go out for lunch. She has cooked for me, though, pork chops and potatoes and some late-summer string beans, and we sit at the kitchen table under the chiming clock as the summer sunlight slants in through the living room windows. The dog sleeps and shuffles his feet on the floor; she feels badly that the taxi was not there when I arrived, and that the driver smoked so much, and did not know how to get to Joanna. "I feel badly I couldn't get you myself," she says, and insists on reimbursing me for the cab. I refuse at first, let the twenty lie on the table between us, but when she gets up and moves away I slip it into my pocket.

"It's not your fault," I offer, but this does not console her. She *has* been driving—out to the mailbox and back every few days, to keep her skills sharp, and is still hopeful that she will be able to regain her doctor's permission.

"When did he say you could drive again?" I ask.

"When I get stronger, whatever that means. We'll see. But tomorrow, if you don't mind, you can drive us over to shop in Morgantown, if you can bear it."

"Sure." I clear the table and start to wash the dishes, and she goes into the living room and settles down into the familiar chair to watch *Jeopardy*. It is in this chair, I have been told, that she sometimes falls asleep and spends the entire night; other times when she cannot sleep, she comes down and spends the night there anyway, sitting up in the darkness and listening to the clock chime, petting the dog's head, afraid to go back upstairs to bed for fear she will never make it down again. She has told all this to my sister, called her more than once to talk, and tell her she was afraid. "Of what?" I had asked, foolishly.

"Death, I suppose," my sister said, shrugging her shoulders. "We talked for an hour. It was wild, Thomas. She made me cry." But my grandmother has never revealed this side of herself to me, and when I go into the living room she is cheerful, amused by some pale-faced accountant from Ohio who is cleaning up on *Jeopardy* and reminds her of a second or third cousin who used to live over in the next county. Afterward, she says good night and goes creaking up the stairs to bed, and I make it halfway through a nature show about wolves and deer before I, too, give up, and step out-side to look at the stars and smell the country air. From over on Route 10, I can hear the passing of cars, the insistent, encroaching whine of civilization. When we first came here as children, the road was still unpaved—a rutted track of packed red earth that released a plume of roiling dust in the wake of passing cars. The road was then paved, and not long after the Amish man who lived at the foot of the hill sold his farm to developers, a stripe of pavement was laid across the potato field, and soon thereafter split-level houses sprouted up like mushrooms. Within a few months grass on the front lawns began to grow, and it took on the look of a street that had always been there. She accepted these changes stoically, though bemoaning the day when not a single light could be seen from the back door.

As children we had come here once a year, making the long drive from New England on a single summer day—eight hours of turnpikes and thruways with all of us packed into our overheated station wagon—two parents, four chil-dren, a single, salivating dog. Toward the end of our journey we stopped in New Jersey somewhere to buy saltwater taffy and to pee, and then pressed on the final hour or two to the farm—across the Delaware River, along the Pennsylvania Turnpike until we saw the familiar smokestack that signaled our exit, and then winding the final few miles to the farm. As we pulled in across the lawn my grandfather would be sitting on the green wooden bench under the chestnut tree, shucking corn, and my grandmother would wave from the back door, releasing two barking dogs, and with our varied suitcases we were ushered into the house, which somehow absorbed us all, two at a time, into double beds, one of us taking turns sleeping with my grandfather in the barn, where he stayed during our visit.

We would spend the day taking the dogs for walks, picking strawberries up in the field, getting poison ivy on the soles of our feet and hay fever so bad that when I woke up in the mornings, my eyes would be glued shut and I had to soak them open with a hot facecloth. We took a lot of long, hot drives to do errands, and to visit second and third cousins who wanted to say hello to my father and have a look at his offspring, and after we had had enough of country life we would pile back into the car for the arduous drive back to New England.

But when I was fifteen, these family trips abruptly ended: not only had we all become too large and fractious to spend eight hours in the car together, but my grandfather had died of a heart attack when I was fourteen, and thereafter my father came to visit my grandmother by plane, and usually alone. For several years, I had not come here at all. When I graduated from college I moved to New York, but after a couple of months of subways and pavement and long, jobless city days, I would start plotting my escape; New England was too far, and going home seemed an admission of failure, but there was a bus that left from Port Authority several times a day and arrived in Reading three hours later. Every few months I would call her to announce an impending visit. "Thank you, Thomas," she would say, in hanging up, and the following morning I would board the bus and watch the city recede—skyscrapers giving way to the low industrial marshes of New Jersey, suburbs yielding to farms and the small, gritty cities of eastern Pennsylvania. Her car would always be there, waiting by the curb, her penumbra of white hair rising up from the driver's seat. Then we would set off with her at the wheel, steering us through the

Pennsylvania countryside with a confidence that I, as a passenger, did not share. She had invested the car with free will, saw driving as a collaboration between its needs and desires and her own: "It wants to take us into the ditch!" she would suddenly announce, as if she had no say in the matter, and sure enough, the wheels on my side would slide off onto the shoulder, kicking up stones and dust with the sound of a crashing wave, veering toward the woods before she managed to wrestle it back onto the pavement. Her driving was informed by remembered bits of automotive wisdom of her husband, long since dead. "Your grandfather used to say you should never brake going down this hill," the car gathering speed down the long, steep descent below the steel mill, sweeping around a long, slowing curve through the woods, rising up a hill toward Goffstown. Our velocity bore no relation to the topography or to the laws of physics, and she tended to accelerate in places I would brake, and vice versa, and out of the corner of her eye she would notice that I was instinctively stomping the floor with my foot. "Now don't get nervous. We're doing the best we can." Sometimes she would ask me to drive, sending the keys skidding across the roof of the car with a jaunty flip of her wrist, and then it was her turn to be nervous, emitting little sighs of terror and suppressed recommendations as we drove, punctuated by reports of automotive catastrophe. "This is the spot where the young Beiber boy was killed," she'd tell me, pointing to a high, steep embankment of weeds that rose up, suddenly, beside the road. "He skidded on the ice, they say, and rolled over five times. His mother went to school with my cousin Sep. He was twenty-two, just finished college. A little younger than you, I think."

But the car was her lifeline, the only thing between her and the Shady Maple Rest Home we would pass on our way to Amish country. As long as she could drive—get over to Birdsboro to buy food for the cats, or over the valley and into the next county to have lunch with a group of women with literary inclinations, or to her appointment with Dr. Shippen, who would tell her, among other things, how her heart was doing and whether her eyes and reflexes were still working well enough for her to drive for another year—she would be all right.

On the morning of my visit we climb into the car early, with me at the wheel, and head off on our rounds—over the hill, past the Shady Maple Rest Home, down past the place where her second-cousin spinsters, Anna and Marie Geiger, used to live, across the beautiful valley of farms, Amish children walking the sun baked road, and across Route 10 to Farmer Brown's. For the first time, she sends me in with a shopping list and stays behind in the car. "Really?" I ask, though I don't mind, because it will be faster; but when I get back to the car she is sitting in the half-open door, looking out over the fields.

"Are you all right?"

"Oh, yes, I'm fine," she says. "Just trying to enjoy the sunshine." A warm late-summer wind is blowing, sweeping through the rattling corn, and as I'm getting back into the car an abandoned shopping cart lets loose and starts rolling across the parking lot, gathering speed, and then crashes into the side of a parked car, bouncing backward. "Well, for goodness' sakes," my grandmother says, not uncheerfully. In the sunlight we can see a small dent the shopping cart has left in the door. "That's too bad."

"It wasn't *our* shopping cart, though," I report.

"Wasn't it?" she says, smiling, suggesting she has already figured this into her moral equation, but adds, a new lightness in her voice, "Gooood."

It is getting hot and I am eager to get back to the farm, but there are other errands to do: down to the shopping center in Knauers for an early lunch, and on the way home, if I don't mind, we can stop at a place in Birdsboro where she has commissioned a lady to make a quilt for me and the woman whom, it has been announced, I will one day marry. I turn left onto Route 20, heading down through the farms and shopping malls and gaudy motels for the tourists who come down to look at the Amish.

At the Blue Bell Diner I turn off and drive slowly through the parking lot and drop her off by the door and park, and when I come back she is leaning up against the brick of the restaurant with her eyes closed, looking pale. "Are you all right?" I ask, and without answering she reaches into her pocketbook and takes a pill—nitroglycerin. She has been advised to have an angioplasty, but she doesn't think blowing up a balloon in an eighty-four-year-old heart is a good idea; but without it, she reports, her breathing will get no better and she should not expect to live "forever."

"My breath just gets a little short, sometimes." I hold her arm as we pass through the door, and she sits at a table while I wait in line and get our food—sausage and mashed potatoes for me, and for my grandmother only a bowl of soup and a piece of pie. "That's all you want?" I ask.

"For now. I'll eat more for dinner, I think." Her loss of appetite is alarming in one who has always loved food. Eating—"gluttony," as she calls it—is the accepted sin in this part of the world, and I am struck by the largeness of the people around us—soft, pale arms bulging out of their shirts, enormous piles of food taken into these soft Germanic faces.

My stays have grown shorter in recent visits, and as we eat I wait for a moment to tell her I can stay for only one day, and will have to leave in the morning, and get back to the bus station in Reading somehow—another riddle. But when I finally tell her she doesn't seem surprised.

"And which bus would you like to catch?" she asks. When I tell her the early one, at seven, she slowly nods. "I wish I could drive you myself, but we'll work something out." I try to apologize for not staying longer, but she takes it all in stride. "No, no. You have your own life to live. This has been a great help, just getting these groceries. And if you can bear it, we can stop off at Mrs. Zorn's place on the way home and look at that quilt I talked about for your wedding present. Then I'll feel as though we've done everything I've wanted, and maybe I can sleep better."

"You didn't sleep well?"

"At first, but I woke up at three, and couldn't get back to sleep after that, and so I came downstairs to read."

"Three?" I ask, but she only nods, gravely. She has always been attuned to the urgency that some of us feel when trying to leave the farm—the agoraphobia of the city people. A couple of years before my moment of departure coincided with the arrival of a snowstorm, and even then my grandmother insisted on trying to get me to the bus station. "We don't want you to get snowed in on the farm, now, do we? I know how city people get when they're trapped down here." In the morning, the wind was blowing hard, and a few flakes had started to fall, and the barn doors crashed back and forth in the wind, as in *The Wizard of Oz* before the tornado. Snow swirled in the twin cones of her headlights, and by the time we got to the bus snow covered the ground. "Are you going to make it back?" I asked her jocularly.

"I think so," she said, and I watched her growl away through the swirling snow. When I got to New York I called. "It was an adventure," she said, "but I made it. We've got about six or eight inches here now. When it stops, I'll get the Weavers to come plow me out."

But that had been in the days before her heart "went bad," when she still mowed the lawn, and cut the lower field with the tractor, and carried cat food and water down to the barn. She is weaker now, and can't make it down to the barn without stopping to lean on the pear tree for a few minutes to rest.

"We'll get you there, somehow," she repeats, and then adds, excited, "Wasn't that something the way that shopping cart crashed into the side of the car? I guess it didn't like the way it was sitting there, shining so nicely in the sun." She laughs, blood flooding up into her face.

When we get to Mrs. Zorn's I walk her to the door, and only then do I detect her new lightness—the absence of her former mass. It is the first time she has been so thin since she was a teenager, before the birth of my father—her only child.

"Rebecca!" Mrs. Zorn says, with a slight lift in her voice. I am surprised to be reminded of her first name. She is of the same age, but of a different type—lighter boned, quick on her feet, twitchy—the kind of woman my grandmother has always been suspicious of, who has always made her nervous. Mrs. Zorn's living room is quietly crowded—a soft, tufted carpet; knickknacks and figurines; a weak light leaking through the curtains; the ticking of a clock. On the couch there is the "crazy quilt" she has been working on—random, geometric shapes of cloth, all stitched together with a zigzagging pattern of thread.

"You see," she tells me, speaking quickly, holding up the quilt, "I get the pieces from all different places, old clothes and worn-out things, even some quilts, and coats, and then I sew it all together to make something—something out of nothing, you might say. That's what I like about it. Make something out of nothing," she repeats, and laughs. She too is frail, and as we move around the house my grandmother lightly holds her arm.

"Do you like it?" my grandmother asks me.

"I do," I say, trying not to sound unenthusiastic. "Do you make any without that zigzagging thread?" I ask, and she looks down at the quilt, and then back at me.

"Oh no," she says gravely. "That's the style."

"That's fine," I say. "I was just wondering." But my grandmother has picked up on my not so hidden meaning, and outside in the car, as we start on down Route 10 back toward the farm, she presses me on it.

"No, I like it," I insist, though in truth I prefer the quilt that covers her own bed, geometric patterns of rectangles in more concordant shades of purple and blue. "And you'll be able to remember where Mrs. Zorn lives?" she asks ominously. "In case I'm not around to help you?"

"You'll be around." I laugh, and then add, "Anyway, I'll remember." Though I privately wonder if Mrs. Zorn will be able to finish the quilt, and my grandmother, as if she has read my thoughts, says quietly, "She has heart problems too."

By the time we get back to the farm it is almost two, and a heavy summer torpor has settled over the place. She lies down on the couch to rest and I go outside for a walk— down across the yard to the stable, empty now, save for the cats that crouch in the cool of the shadows by the sandstone walls, and the old Ford tractor that sits in the now deserted stable where the horse once lived. I have always wanted to drive the tractor and mow the field, but her suspicion of my driving has extended to her farm machinery, and whenever I have offered she has found a reason to discourage me—the grass is too wet, or it isn't yet long enough for cutting, or she has promised the job to the son of her second cousin Earl—and so for my rural experience I settle for mowing the lawn, sweeping back and forth across the yard on her small riding mower, up and around the house, weaving in and out of the several rows of pine trees my grandfather planted thirty years before as Christmas trees; she became so fond of them that she dissuaded her husband from cutting them down, and now they are forty feet tall and unfit for selling.

But even my lawn mowing is suspect, and before my most recent effort she had told me to keep the mower in second gear. "Now, I know young people have trouble going slowly," she said gently, "but I think second is the right gear. If you go too fast, it doesn't cut right, and you put a strain on the engine." And so I set off, mowing smooth, broad swaths across the lawn, but, true to her prediction, I grew impatient with the snail's pace of second gear, and when I thought I was out of sight, on the blind side of the house, I would slip it into third, race along for ten or twenty yards, and then downshift into second when I came back into view. A couple of weeks before, she mowed it herself, as a way of keeping her driving skills sharp until she is allowed to drive her car again.

On a previous visit I had helped her pull some old, rotted fence poles out of the ground and replace them with new ones—a task she had described, before I began, as being too difficult for "one man." But I had insisted, and after a protracted struggle I finished the job, at which point she admitted that the way you could get a man to do something was to tell him he couldn't do it by himself.

"Really?" I looked at her and laughed.

"You didn't know that?"

"I do now—it worked."

She has left me with no assignment today, and she is inside, sleeping, and so I walk up around the barn and up the road, up to the end of Weaver Road and then down along another that runs between her fields and the neighbor's farm. They rent her land, grow corn and strawberries and potatoes, and in the last couple years have planted several rows of fruit trees along the lower edge of the field. They asked her permission first, and she is grateful for the change, she has told me, as it keeps the topsoil from her land from washing over the road and into the Weavers' pond.

The road slopes down to a swale in the land and then rises up between the woods and the field, where the developers built new houses, small, each surrounded by an acre of scruffy, woodsy land, the lawns not yet taken to grass. "I don't mind sharing the woods with the city people, just so long as they don't use up all the water that runs off Red Hill. I'm just not so sure there's enough for all of us." Her environmentalism long preceded the environmentalists, the people who show up at her back door, more and more, wondering what, once she is gone, she intends to do with her land, asking if she would like to give it over to the conservation people or put a lien on it to prevent development; but to do so, she has discovered, she must also leave a large endowment to maintain it, which she does not have. My father doesn't want her to protect it, on the grounds that it would "bite" into his grandchildren's inheritance, but I've told her we have enough of an inheritance already. She would like one of us to come live here, take over the farm that has been in the family for one hundred years, but that, too, is not likely: we are visitors, city people, and the countryside is turning into something else, sprouting up with houses and industrial complexes and malls; and what would we do here, without her to show us the way? My father, knows all this already, and has told her that when the "time comes," he would like to sell the house and barn and the twenty acres they sit on, and keep the remaining fifty across the road for us. I have told her to do with it what *she* wants, and if she wants to put a lien on it she should, but since her heart troubles began she no longer has the energy to call up lawyers and conservation people, nor the energy to defy her only child.

"Who will feed the birds?" she asked me once, looking at me with a sad, stricken look which, in a recognition of the pathos of her concern, dissolved into a smile. "They'll be all right, I guess. City people have bird feeders, don't they?"

To the woods behind the house, hunters come in fall, with guns and bows and arrows, and now and then one of their bullets goes whizzing over the house or ricochets off the barn, and she would sometimes run into one of the hunt-ers as they cut across the yard and have a brief conversation, the nuances and inflections of which she would mull over for days. She does not much care for hunters or hunting, but gives them permission to hunt on her land, accepting them as a part of the natural scheme of things, a rung on a peck-ing order it is not her place to dislodge.

And recently, hang gliders have begun to appear over the field with the high-pitched whine of lawn mowers: this, too, she observes with a kind of bemused curiosity, another miracle of the modern world, only worrying that one of them will fall into her field like Icarus.

"Then what will I do? I read in the *Reading Eagle* that when they're up there they feel like they're a part of nature." She cradled her forehead in her hand. "As if we're not all a part of nature already."

When I get back to the house she is sitting in her chair in the living room; her eyes are closed, and her hair is down, spread out across her shoulders like a shawl. I stand for a minute behind her, to see if she is breathing.

"I've been trying to think how we can get you to the bus station tomorrow," she says, startling me. "I tried to call Pastor Snyder, but there was no answer—he may be up in Muhlenberg at a conference, as I remember."

"I can take a taxi, like I got here."

"But what if he smokes, like the last one? And talks too much?"

"I can take it—it's only a few minutes."

"Maybe I can take you myself," she suggests, but I don't take her seriously.

"Didn't the doctor say you might be able to drive again soon?"

"No, he didn't. He said we'll see after my next appoint-ment."

"And when will that be?"

"In the middle of the month. We'll figure something out."

And then at dinner she says casually, "I'll take you to the bus station myself, I think. Pastor Snyder isn't home yet, and I don't think you should be taking a taxi. What if they don't come on time, or smoke too much?"

"But you're not supposed to drive, are you?"

"That's what the doctor says, but he's not the police; I still have my license. And now and then I've been driving down to get dog and cat food, and to church. It will be Sunday morning, and I'll be back before eight. I don't think there will be much traffic. And if you're willing to take us over, I'll save my strength for the drive back."

"Really?" I'm torn between my desire to get to the bus on time and concern for her safety on the return. But driving may give her "a boost," help her get back on the road, and who am I to say no? She adds, "It will be an adventure."

She has cooked again, but she is eating only a small bowl of chicken soup and a honey bun she has smuggled back from the Blue Bell. She has been told not to drink coffee, but after dinner we have some anyway, instant, that she drinks with some of her pills. "Thank you for driving me around and getting the groceries," she says, finally. "That's a big load off my mind. And you won't forget where Mrs. Zorn lives, now, will you, in case I'm not there to show you?"

I laugh it off, but then add, "I think so."

On my last few visits she has taken to asking me which of her possessions I like and would like to have "someday." I am reluctant to make a claim on anything, but, not wanting to displease her or, for that matter, miss my chance at ownership, I have confessed a fondness for the tile of the Dutch boy my grandfather bought in Trenton, New Jersey, and for some of the tools in the barn. "Do you still like the chair in the corner?" she asks, about a large armchair with a floral design. But of this chair she once said, "You know, everyone who's ever sat in that chair isn't with us anymore.

And you know whose been sitting in it lately? Your father."
But it looks too big for my house. "And the quilt, of course,"
she says, "when Mrs. Zorn is finished."

I clear the table and wash the few dishes, but she is too
tired even to watch TV. She puts some food out for the cats
and gives me more to take down to the barn, and then goes
up to bed, the sound of her feet creaking up the stairs. Halfway, she stops and says, "I'll wake you up around six or so,
if you don't mind."

Outside, the late-summer moon is full—the harvest
moon, she calls it—and a warm wind is blowing up from
the south. Down in the barn I can hear moving cats and see
pairs of gleaming copper eyes. I walk up around the barn to
the road and look out across the moonlit fields of corn to
the woods, where I can see a few twinkling lights of the city
people. The dog hobbles along behind me, but she has grown
too fat to run. We walk slowly back to the house, where she
settles with a sigh on the floor, and I watch an old movie
with Jimmy Stewart in one of his less memorable roles, and
resist the urge to go through some old photo albums, mem-
orializing the past. Every half hour the clock chimes, and
when it sounds ten, I succumb to the rich country air and
creak upstairs to bed.

In the morning I wake on my own, when a reddish blur
has appeared on the horizon. A few persistent stars still
hang in the cobalt blue sky. Downstairs she has her coat on
already, and has set out a place for me at table. "Now you're
sure you still want to do this?" I ask.

"I'm still game, if you're willing." After a hurried bowl
of cereal and a not so hot cup of instant coffee we go out,
my grandmother handing me the keys and then moving
around to the passenger's side, holding on to the car for sup-
port. Birds are singing, and a low orange light is falling on
dewy grass. A single black cat stares out at us from under a
boxwood bush—bad luck. I start the car and let it warm up,

as she would, and then back slowly out across the grass, up by the barn, take a final look at the house, and then pull out down the road.

Traffic is light, and I drive quickly, rising and falling along the empty road—down past the church, the cemetery, the softball field, past the gun shop I had been to once as a child, past the new condominium complex and golf course where a few elderly-looking types are out early, leaving trails of footprints in the dew. She slept well, she tells me, and is cheerful, talkative—happy to be up and out in the car, perhaps, defying Dr. Shippen's orders. In the early-morning light even the gritty factories and rusting bridges and empty boxcars on the outskirts of Reading are beautiful, and the short, stolid skyscrapers rise up out of the morning mist like monuments to some other, more hopeful time.

I turn off the highway and follow her directions to the bus station—a succession of left-hand turns through what has become, in recent years, a Puerto Rican and Dominican neighborhood. At a red light I hear her laugh to herself, and when I ask her what it is she points to a small variety store on a corner where my grandfather used to visit. "He liked to go in there and talk. There was a man there who was willing to listen to him, until one day he had had enough of your grandfather's wisdom, I guess, and said something, and your grandfather left and never went back."

"Really? What did he say?" I ask.

"He never did tell me. Maybe he asked if he was ever going to buy anything." Her face has turned red in amusement, and she laughs again, cradling her forehead. "Whatever it was, it was something your grandfather couldn't bring himself to forgive."

The light turns red and I creep down the last block to the bus station, and beside me she is still remembering, shaking her head. "Well, for goodness' sakes."

I pull into the familiar spot beside the "No Standing" sign, turn off the car, and lean over and kiss her on the cheek good-bye. "Have a nice drive back," I say, handing over the keys, trying to sound upbeat.

"Oh, I will, I'll try my best. And thanks for everything, Thomas. I appreciate all your help." I wait until she slides over into the driver's seat, looking like her old self, and then, not wanting to put her under undo scrutiny, I turn and go into the station. There is no line, but by the time I have my ticket and look back outside, the Skylark and my grandmother are gone.

I had no idea at the time that within a month I would be back, not to visit my grandmother but to bury her—help carry her casket up to the familiar family plot in the cemetery to join her husband and parents and various relatives we used to visit together. She had died suddenly, her entire, diminished mass crashing to the kitchen floor like a statue, smashing her eyeglasses, the car keys she had been holding skidding across the floor. She had her coat on, and was about to drive over to Birdsboro for a tune-up: she had still not received permission to drive again, but was determined to be ready when she did.

I have since wondered if it wasn't some sort of divine intervention that caused her heart to stop then and there, in the safety of her own house, and not out on Route 10, where she might have taken someone else with her. Or perhaps it was, simply, the apprehension and excitement of the journey that caused her heart to speed up, and then stop altogether. In any case, I like to think of her as happy at that moment, looking forward to getting the car ready, and herself back on the road.

I didn't know that among her possessions to come my way, along with the tile and the tools and the large floral armchair, would be the car itself—her own white Buick Skylark. It was not in her will, but my siblings decided that I—

with a child on the way and soon to be married—was in greater need of one than they were, and it now sits outside my house, crouching, waiting. When I first got it, it still held the fragrance of the farm, but with time even this faded, leaked away through the cracks into the odorless New England air. I never did make it back for the crazy quilt, and settled instead for the one that always lay on my grandmother's bed—of a more regular pattern of purple and blue and gold.

Within a year the farm as I knew it was also gone, its remaining contents dispersed at auction and the twenty acres, house, and barn sold to a second cousin of whom, my father reported, my grandmother was not overly fond. A month later half of the barn roof blew off in a freak tornado that swept across the township, vindicating my father's decision to sell the place, but I like to think it was my grandmother who had returned, in the form of a high and angry wind, to wreak havoc on her second cousin. True to his promise, my father hung on to the remaining fifty acres for our inheritance, and continues to rent it out to the Weavers—the last working farm in the township. I would like to visit sometime, and look out across the empty field, but when, and with whom, and where to go afterward, for lunch?

Rather, it is our final drive together I like to remember—the empty road before us, the dappled sunlight slanting in through the trees, the passing factories and farms, the hopeful and daring prospect of my grandmother driving home alone, getting better. And there is the lingering pleasantness of the final laugh—the tale of my grandfather getting his feelings hurt, and her amusement at the memory. I was at the wheel, it is true, but it was she who got us there and got herself back, and as we swept over the soft, familiar landscape of the past, she seemed happy beside me, airborne at last.

A Word with the Boy

We had arrived in London that morning, after an all-night flight from America. My wife had met us at the airport and led us through the throngs of summer travelers to the underground that would take us into the city, to the dormitory room where, for this summer month, she had been staying. "You're dressed alike," she had said, smiling, and it was true. We were both wearing khaki pants, and at the last minute back at the house, as we waited for a taxi to take us to the airport, William had run upstairs for his button-down cotton shirt, like the one I was wearing. He had been happy all day, in anticipation of the journey, of seeing his mother, and when we left, finally, he insisted on carrying his own bags, a blue knapsack and the sleeping bag I had bought him for his eighth birthday.

On the train ride in from Heathrow I kept almost falling asleep, winking and nodding in the early-morning sunlight that kept flashing through the car. Across the aisle a young woman was watching us fight off sleep, vaguely smiling as she worked out the simple genetic equation to herself: beige man + brown woman = handsome light brown boy. But William looks, people say, more like me than his mother—same skin tone, same shaped face, and hair closer to straight than curly. He is a handsome boy, as well as a sensitive one, and we have been assured he will be a "heartbreaker" when he gets older, but it is his own heart I am worried about—the hurts he may suffer at the hands of precocious adolescent girls. Even now, at the age of eight, he spends his days by the stereo, listening to the love songs that float into our house from the wounded hearts of crooning teenage singers.

I had been looking after him for nearly a month while his mother attended a summer institute on "postcolonial literature" here in London. The day before, he had packed his bag early and then waited happily all day in front of the television set as I frantically prepared for our departure, and when the moment had come, finally, we dodged a sudden summer thunderstorm, got a ride to the subway with a neighbor, and took three different trains and one shuttle bus to the terminal. All the way he had insisted on carrying his own bags—one on his back, the other effortfully hoisted along through the subway stations, up an escalator, through a turnstile, and onto a bus, and then through the cool interior spaces of the airport. When we got on the plane, finally, he had slept for much of the flight, his head resting on my shoulder as we drifted through the strange intercontinental twilight—an edge of summer brightness never quite leaving the curve of the northern horizon—waking only long enough to eat before falling back into his deep boyhood sleep.

Our time alone together had been easier than I had expected. He has reached the age of friendships and playmates and has begun to navigate the several blocks to school on his own. He had surprised me, further, by seldom mentioning his mother, but he hugged me more than usual, and sometimes when walking down the street, if no one was around to see, he would spontaneously hold my hand, letting go only if someone his own age appeared. In his mother's absence, our own relationship had taken on some of the emotional tonality of the maternal. He rarely cries anymore, and when he does it is usually for reasons of physical rather than emotional pain, squeezing back the tears as soon as he is able. But now, on our subway ride into the city, to the dormitory where we will be staying, it is *her* shoulder he is sleeping on, not mine, and I suspect it will be to her that he now gravitates in moments of hurt, leaving me to drift back to the more recessed roles of fatherhood.

We changed trains once at Green Street, lugged our bags up and down a maze of stairways and escalators, through the peculiar though not unpleasant scent of the London underground, and then rose up into the bright, mottled daylight of morning, walked two blocks through the streets of London, and took an elevator up to the room. Exhausted, we shed our clothes, and I climbed in under the covers and he into his unfurled sleeping bag, and fell into a deep, jet-lagged sleep.

I had lived here once before, for a year, when I was twelve, and part of my hope for our visit is to show him something of my own childhood haunts: the house where we lived overlooking the vast green reaches of Regent's Park, the paths I used to traverse on my way to school, the lush fields where I first began to play soccer, a sport that he, too, has taken to. I was only twelve when we arrived that fall thirty years ago, but had soon learned how to catch the bus on the street behind our house and ride it down into central London by myself, wandering through the cold and the crowds of Oxford Street, breaking into a sprint, now and then, for no particular reason, dodging pedestrians like an American football star, ducking into department stores, until, finally, in the dark of a winter evening, I would buy a bag of hot chestnuts from the grizzled hawker with blackened fingers and smuggle it up to the top of the bus, warming my hands as I slowly ate them. This was 1968, and the Vietnam War was in full swing, and anti-American sentiment was palpable, even to a twelve-year-old boy with nicely cut hair. One felt unpopular out on the streets, and I was always reluctant to speak and reveal my American voice. But I fell in love with soccer on the vast open reaches of Regent's Park, and then with a pretty freckled girl from Texas in the American school that we attended, and I have continued to revisit the city with a nostalgic fondness and a vague sense of entitlement, an honorary citizen returned. Compared to America, with our hot summer streets and our guns and our simmering history of violence and race, England has always seemed a safer and benign place, where even crime takes on a certain quaintness—a retiring gentleman in Sussex is "taken in" for fertilizing his garden with the diced remains of his half sister. But the English television shows we watch back home have begun to take on a darker edge—creepy urban hoodlums and corrupt policemen converging in gritty urban "estates" that are anything but quaint. And often in these programs are undertones of racial and cultural conflict that we Americans have always claimed as our own special province.

When I wake, the boy is already up, nattering happily around the room, and his mother is preparing to go out to an afternoon seminar and will be back by dinnertime—we're on our own again. I wake groggily, eat the sandwiches she has made for us, take a bath in an enormous tub, and then we go outside for a walk. There, the morning sun has given way to low gray clouds interspersed with lower, faster-moving ones, and the sidewalks are mottled with patches of damp and darker gray, with a rain that must have fallen while we slept. But everything seems busier than I remember it, and the red buses of my childhood have been plastered with garish billboards, and some of the taxis have been painted improbable shades of purple or red. The cars don't seem to stop or slow for pedestrians, and I hold his arm tightly as we try to get across the street, concentrating hard to figure out which way they are coming from. Half the people on the street, it seems, are talking into tiny portable telephones—"mobiles," they call them here.

We drift slowly down Tottenham Court Road, and I try to remember what it is famous for. The insides of the phone booths, I notice, are plastered with pictures of nearly naked women, and phone numbers to call. I would like to look closer but, in deference to the boy, resist. We walk some more, and pause in front of a store featuring hundreds of Swiss Army knives, all opened to reveal their countless multipurpose blades. How much do they cost, he wants to know, but I plead ignorance and prod us along the street. Then there is a video game place, full of bleeping, blaring machines, small boys intently driving skidding, tumbling race cars. This, too, I resist, and we wander as far as some handsome "American Church" that I seem to remember from a previous visit, and we turn and walk back up the sidewalk. I hurry us past the video arcade, but there is something about all those gleaming blades and devices that captivates even me, and we drift over to study them some more.

"Let's go," I say, and turn, and that's when I notice the two hatted men walking slowly toward us, closing in: policemen of some sort, though not bobbies with their jolly, comic cone hats, but a more modern, up-to-date, and vaguely sinister style that I recognize from English detective shows. I keep expecting them to veer off, toward some more worthy target, but they don't, and keep walking slowly, inexorably toward us. And then one of them is talking to us, in soft, not unkindly tones—something about how they noticed us "walking about," asking us where we are from, what we are doing here, where we are staying, what is my "relationship" to the boy. They noticed that we are "different colors," he offers in explanation.

"I'm his father," I say, and then point around the corner toward the dorm where we are staying, but I can't quite remember the name; I tell him we are here to visit his mother—my wife—who is attending a six-week institute at the university. We just arrived that morning. He explains that there are a lot of lost or runaway boys in the neighborhood, "begging and the like," and sometimes they fall in with the wrong men, and would we mind if they have a word with the boy—"separately," he asks, nodding to the side. I don't have the presence of mind to say no, that I do mind, that you can talk to both of us here if you want but not separately, and say "Okay" instead. Then his partner takes William a few feet away, and while one asks me a few simple questions—what's my first name and what street do we live on back in America—I listen to the other one asking my son the same questions, and his quiet, resolute answers. And then it is all quietly over, we are reunited, father and son, and one of them says "Thank you," and then they just drift away, down the street, and leave us in a strange, unsettling limbo.

"Come on," I say, wanting to get away from this street that suddenly seems unclean, "let's go over to that park we saw," but he doesn't answer, and we walk in silence, mulling over what has just happened. I don't want to speak until I can figure out what he has made of it all, or what I have made of it myself. I wonder how much of it he has picked up on—the part about being "different colors." Couldn't they see that we are dressed alike, hear that we talk alike, that we both have American accents? The whole thing evolved so quietly, so slowly, I didn't have the wherewithal to put a stop to their inquest, to refuse to have my son taken aside, pulled away from his own father to be questioned, at the age of eight, by the police. Too late.

We walk a few blocks in silence and come upon a small cement soccer field with two goals made out of pipe at either end. "I want to go home," he says finally.

"Back to the dorm?" I ask hopefully.

"No. Back to America. I don't like it here."

"The policemen, you mean?"

"Exactly."

"Ah—don't worry about them," I say, but I have not yet formed a full explanation.

We walk some more and find another park, with grass this time, where a few people on lunch hour are sitting around, eating and talking. We go in through the main entrance and sit on a small hill where I find a white feather on the grass with a modest magical property: when dropped from a certain height, it turns sideways against the air and then spins slowly to the ground like a maple seed.

"Hey, let me see that," he says, brightening, and then he plays with it for a while, throwing it up in the air and watching it spin downward, trying to catch it before it lands. But across the park there are two Indian men who seem to be watching us intently.

"Why are those two men staring at us?" he wants to know.

"They like watching us play," I say, unconvinced that this is the reason. He plays some more with the feather, and I am hoping it will purge the aftertaste of our encounter with the policemen and restore his good humor. We keep it for good luck, but on our way out of the park, back toward our motherless room, he repeats his request.

"I want to go home."

"Why?"

"I don't like it here. The people aren't nice."

"Ah, Willy—you can't let two silly policemen ruin your whole day. They're just trying to protect . . ." I say but can't quite finish the sentence: protect whom? Boys from their own fathers? "There are a lot of runaway kids around here," I say, aping the policemen, but what about my son looks like a runaway boy, and why would they not think I am his father? At the back of my mind is the knowing that I, too, am culpable—should have refused, should have shown a little courage, or outrage, or defiance, should not have allowed this symbolic act of separation, of my son being taken away by the police for questioning. But it was such a gentle act of violence—yes, that is the right word—that I didn't know what was happening until it was over.

"They're just trying to protect children," people would explain to us later, an explanation that is of little use now, or later.

"I want to go home," he repeats when we return, tired and diminished, to the room, our month alone together ancient history. Our bags are still strewn around in disarray, and I start to unpack, and he throws himself down onto the bed, exhausted—that's all—from our night of flying: after a little nap, he'll be himself again. I hang my clothes in the closet, and unpack his into two drawers that slide out from under the bed. I put the suitcases away in the closet, straighten the covers, and look over to see if he has fallen asleep. He is still there, in his nice, rumpled travel clothes, but he has turned his face away from me, and has pulled the collar of his shirt to his eyes—to block out the light, I'd like to think, but it's not true. I sit down on the bed beside him and lay my hand on his back. I can tell that he is not asleep, and has pulled up his shirt to hide from me his own tears.

"What's the matter?" I ask, panicking now. "What is it?" I rub his small, strong back, but he does not—or cannot—answer: there are no words for what the matter is, for what has hurt him, and I, too, give up on explanation. I lie down on the bed beside him, drape my arms around him, and he turns and pulls me back toward him with the fierce grip of a wounded lover. And for the first time in our summer month together, he cries in earnest, his hurt released in short, breathless sobs, tears flowing freely now as he gives himself over to sorrow and weeps in my arms like a child.

Kinds of Love

It wasn't easy, getting out of the house these early Sunday mornings, and Daniel went about his morning rituals with a quiet sense of urgency—a nervous, overly deliberate energy: making the coffee, doing some paperwork for the coming week, washing a few dishes and tidying up the kitchen, then delivering the Sunday paper and coffee to his wife, still stirring in the nest of their shared bed. He had already done a load of laundry, washed and dried his own clothes, then hung them on hangers for the coming week. The child, a girl, was still in bed, soon to wake—hopefully soon so he could talk to her for a moment before it was time to leave.

And then there was the problem of the clothes—the trick of looking half decent when he arrived, but not so well dressed that he drew attention to himself when he returned: a button-down shirt, sweater, decent shoes—a cut above his normal weekend rags—but no coat or tie. Should he carry his shoulder bag with office work, lending credence to the muttered falsity that he was going to do some paperwork at a coffee shop? Not necessary.

It was 8:37, his cell phone told him, and as he sat at his desk, waiting, wondering what else could be done, he heard the thump, thump, thump of the child, seven years old, coming down the stairs, one step at a time, holding a doll and dragging a blanket behind her. "Hi, Jennie," he said, and she came into the room, gave him a tight little hug and kiss on the cheek before passing through the kitchen to the living room for the usual diet of cartoons. "Good night's sleep?" he asked, settling onto the couch beside her.

"Yes."

"Do you need to do anything for school?" He still could not believe they actually gave homework at this age.

"Just to read, and draw some pictures."

"All right," he said. "Watch a little TV first. I'm going out for a little while, then I'll be back. I'll see you in an hour or two." Why did the statement sound like a question? He touched her curly blond hair.

"All right," she said, hugging the doll, then added, "Where are you going?"

"Just for a bike ride and to do a little work, maybe." Then, as if to diminish the weight of the fib, he decided to carry his book bag after all. He pottered around some more, washed a few more dishes, checked the time.

"Okay—bye, bye."

"Bye, Daddy."

"See you soon." He leaned over to kiss her on the cheek good-bye, then called up the stairs to his wife, and he heard the faint reply: "See you later."

The door squeaked as he pressed it open and stepped out into the cool spring air. But there was the yellow cat, thudding up the stairs and scolding him with a shrill meow, and in another, small act of kindness, he opened the door to let her back in. Even the cat was female: his destiny, perhaps, to be surrounded and mystified by members of the opposite sex.

It was always a relief to get out of the house, finally, to break free, for a time, from the bonds of gravity, from the mysterious forces that held them all together, this small constellation of family. Inertia, he seemed to remember, was what?—the impulse of an object to stay at rest, unless otherwise impelled to move by some other stronger force? Or was it the impulse of an object to continue moving in the direction it was already going? Or both?

At the moment, moving, for he had already unlocked his bicycle and was gliding along through the soft, cool air beneath a canopy of leafing trees, the pale green of their unfurling and the yellowish paleness of their tiny flowers. Shifting shapes of pale blue sky appeared through parting clouds, the world made clean and new from last evening's rain. It was April, the ground long since thawed, the world coming back to life.

He made his usual zigzag through the neighborhood—left, right, left, right—across the railroad tracks, and through the buildings of the university, then out onto the larger brightness of the river where a few joggers and walkers were plodding along the pathway, stirring up the Sunday-morning air. He turned right over the bridge, then crossed the river where a few crew shells were neatly splicing the cold blue water like giant, eight-oared insects, leaving an expanding V of wake. He checked his watch—ten minutes to nine still: he would be, as he often was, a few minutes late. It was the only thing, she had once pointed out to him, for which he was not on time.

Across the river he took a sharp left down a "public alley" that ran behind the backs of the chic row houses, all brick and stone. There was something pleasant about passing through this canyon of homes, past their garbage cans and their BMWs and Mercedeses and Range Rovers, still and deserted, save for the occasional dog walkers, the silence broken by their walking feet, or a sudden bark, or the hollow ringing of bells, rolling over the slate roofs and down into his private passageway, summoning the faithful to worship.

He followed the sound, and after a couple more lefts and rights he arrived in the shadow of the church, stolid and dignified, its stonework patterns of light and darker shades of brown. He locked his bike at the meter next to her car, with the broken parking light which, it had often occurred to him, it would have been nice for him to repair.

From inside he could hear the somber drone of the organ, and then the chorus rising upward and pressing through the thick oak doors, drawing him in: he opened them onto a foyer, into the homey warmth particular, he had noticed, to churches of this denomination: always the same red carpet with its patterns of white flowers, walls of polished wood, smooth and dark, a tall cast-iron radiator nearby, giving off the dry and righteous heat of Christian fellowship. He walked silently toward the velvet-curtained entrance, caught a glimpse of the chorus as they filed in, then stood silently against the wall, waiting, trying to make out the muffled words of confession: *"Almighty and most merciful father, we have erred and strayed from thy ways like lost sheep, We have followed too much the devices and desires of our own hearts. We have offended against thy holy laws . . ."* Then it was over, the shuffle and ruffle of the congregation settling down again, and he slipped in, turned to his right, and sat in an empty pew, at right angles to the altar.

He could not see them at first, but then did, a few rows behind their usual spot, partially obscured by a regular—a bald and beautifully suited man, bellowing out the hymn in his well-trained baritone. She was still wearing her coat and a hat he had bought her once, on a business trip to New York, and beside her, her daughter, coloring away on some biblical scene she had been given at the door. They thought of everything, these Episcopalians.

"Glory to God in the highest, and peace to his people on earth. . . . Lord God, lamb of God, you take away the sins of the world: have mercy on us." He did not join in the singing of the canticle, even though he knew some of the words. As a child he had loved to sing, joined in heartily during music class, but then in sixth grade he had tried out for chorus, been "cut," and since then he had been deeply inhibited by the knowledge that he could not carry a tune. Couldn't they have *taught* him, instead of dropping him, snuffing out his love of singing at such an early age? For a time Rachel had encouraged him to try, nudged him lightly with her elbow until he had said, one Sunday, "When the nightingales sing, the frogs should listen." She smiled in apparent agreement, and thereafter had left him alone.

If she noticed that he had arrived she did not let on—continued to stare straight ahead, giving her full attention to the matters at hand, the service and her devotions: pale alabaster skin, pretty pale green eyes. Only her daughter noticed him, finally, waved happily, nudged her mother, and then, remembering that she did not really like him, gave him her squinchy mouse face and smirk and went back to her colorings.

He considered making his move and joining them now after the second reading and before the sermon, but felt too self-conscious, with all the congregation watching, unknown pairs of eyes, people who might know him, and so he would wait until Communion, when there would be a general shuffle of congregants and he could slip in unnoticed. What did he care, anyway, what anybody saw, or thought? You can't blame someone for going to church. He didn't know any of these good worshipers, anyway, although many looked familiar, as if all Episcopalians fit into four or five generic types, each aging in turn, drifting into middle age, then going over the edge, only to be replaced by younger, fitter versions of themselves.

The service moved forward like a ship easing out of port. Why was he not good at paying attention, fully immersing himself in the service? Fragments of the readings would catch his attention, a familiar line or phrase, before his thoughts drifted and strayed: *"But he was wounded for our transgressions, crushed for our iniquities; upon him was the punishment that made us whole, and by his bruises we are healed. All we like sheep have gone astray; we have all turned to our own way, and the Lord has laid on him the iniquity of us all"* (Isaiah 53:5–6). There they were again, those lost sheep. So that's where it had come from, this famous refrain of the Messiah that filled his mother's house on Christmas morning, his sisters joining in. *"Have gone astray-ay, ay-ay-ay-ay,"* then the rising and falling of this final attenuated syllable.

He had been that week, as she liked to put it, "agitated." First one evening he had not been able to reach her on the phone, and she had never called him back: she had fallen asleep on the couch and not woken until four in the morning. He had slept badly, getting up, finally, and taking a fitful walk at 6 a.m., when she had finally called him back, cool and unapologetic. Then over lunch one day, she had flirted unnecessarily with a fellow customer, a dapper businessman sitting alone at another table, and when he left finally, she had said, "Hmm, not bad. No ring—why didn't I meet him first?" He had tried to laugh it off as one of her casual remarks, with teeth, but it had stayed with him all day and into the night, and had caused him, as she liked to say, to "pout." But why did he get so wrought, why so vulnerable to these meaningless particulars of everyday life—her sudden mood swings, her whims of communication, her ability to "shut him out" for a few days and then simply return, as happy as ever?

He was still raw from these abrasions and closed his eyes, sat up, clasped his hands, and tried to "center himself in the middle of his own breathing," as they encouraged in yoga class. He had come to enjoy church for this alone— this hour of attempted centeredness, of sitting still and doing nothing else for this one sacred interlude in the busyness and chaos of the week, the logistics of deception and the roller coaster of his own emotions: home, and then to work, and then the trying and needing to see her, be with her, on phone or in person, in spirit and the flesh, the discontent and apprehensions when he could not, and then home again, back to husbandhood and fatherhood, back into the pretense and sometimes comfort of normalcy.

She, too, had a biblical name: Rachel. He enjoyed observing her from a distance, watching her sing and pray and rise for Communion while he himself just sat, letting the good and the righteous and the devoted file up for the wafer and the wine, then make his chess move—knight to queen four—for the grand finale. But today, with spring in full bloom outside, and the air soft and fragrant, and the warm yellow light filtering through the stained glass, and her, looking so pretty and serene in the thin floral dress that held her body so, and his eagerness and need to make sure that all was still well between them, he decided he could not wait, and so when the matronly Sunday-school lady appeared at the front, before the sermon, and rang her bell, and all the children went up to the front like a school of fish, he took the opportunity to get up also and move, swiftly, down one aisle, back up another, and then into the pew beside her, in the warm spot the child had just vacated, and whispered "Good morning," and she answered, also in a whisper, "Good morning."

He did not yet take her hand as he wanted to, but would

wait; for there was the sonorous reverend, high above him, settling into his sermon after the usual good mornings and muted ecclesiastical witticisms, sending a collective chortle rolling back through the congregation. Daniel closed his eyes and readied himself to pay attention, calmed by the weight of her beside him, the subtle erotic charge he gathered from the fragrance, the warmth of her arm against his. He would try to listen and glean what wisdom he could from the sermon, something to shed light on the precarious state of his heart and body and mind.

His religious upbringing was spotty, at best: Presbyterian in theory, but by the age of eight or nine his parents had given up on dressing him up and forcing them out—he and his siblings—to church, and they had drifted into heathenism. And then for a time he had been loosely affiliated with a motley tribe of Unitarians, and on Sundays he would report to some sort of meetinghouse, play games, draw pictures, and go on overnight camping trips. He could not remember, in any of these meetings, any mention of Jesus, or God, though there was some artwork involved, on a sunlit, coiled rug, of dimly remembered biblical tales.

And all his life he had been friends with a boy whose father, and grandfather, and most of whose uncles, were Episcopalian ministers, and in the summers he would spend a week or two with them at a summerhouse on a lake in Maine, and it was there that he gathered his favorable impressions of church life—the woody warmth of the building itself, nestled amongst the pines, the good-natured fellowship of the parishioners, the dusty cast of characters in the stained-glass windows who sometimes came to life in the readings or sermons, then returned to their frozen state in the colored glass. The service would always end a minute or two before the hour, spilling over only on days when there were a few bawling babies to baptize, or a long line of summer campers waiting to receive the host. But it was the wooden pews he grew fond of, the well-worn red carpeting, the coffee hour afterward with the kids slipping into the recreation hall next door in a state of barely controlled mayhem, neckties or not, for games of basketball and bombardment.

Pretty girls, he had discovered, also went to church, and it was not an unwelcome distraction to watch them during the service, their half-turned faces, the way their hair fell and cascaded down their backs, a blue barrette refracting the beam of sunlight that happened to fall upon it when a girl turned, and diffracting into a fleeting starburst of blue. There was, too, the coy excitement when they walked past him, and afterward, packed into the car with his best friend's two sisters, the pleasant feeling of being cleansed and good, the prospect of tuna fish sandwiches, and the whole long summer afternoon looming before them.

Once a month, though, there was the problem of Communion, of whether he should join them as they rose and filed up to the altar in their solemn procession, the uncertainty of who was supposed to go up, and why, and it was somehow communicated to him that when everyone else in his row stood and filed up to the altar to receive, with cupped hands, the tasteless wafer and sip of wine, he should remain where he was, alone and Godless in the pew. It was always a relief when they returned, happy and renewed, and he became again one of the flock.

Later, in college, he had had a Catholic girlfriend, from a large Italian-Hungarian family on Long Island—featuring several brainy brothers and a trio of starry-eyed, gum-snapping sisters with lithe teenage bodies—and this awkwardness of devotions was reenacted when he went to church with them once or twice, and when the moment of truth came, after a long buildup of the swinging incense and bells and white tablecloths and the golden bowls that held the sacrament, the whole righteous family began to file up to the altar, press past his lapsed-Protestant knees, and as he watched his pretty girlfriend—she of the reddish hair tumbling down her head in waves—it was to the pleasant recollection that only a few hours earlier, she had slipped into his room and, as the first blush of dawn pressed against the window, had wordlessly undressed him with the same tender care of the priest preparing the host, and then had begun her attentions, on his neck, and cheek, and mouth, her own clothes falling away from her until, at last, her pale and naked body was swaying slowly above him, bathed in the milky morning light coming through the curtains, and she had made love to him with a sweet tenderness, their mutual climax celebrated by the distant chiming of bells. Afterward, back in her homey flannel nightgown, she lay in his arms, then stole away to her mother and sisters in the kitchen, joined in the chaste bustle of preparation—a dozen eggs, toast, bacon, everything for the ravenous family. Ah, the sweet complicity of women!

But his visits to this church, going on, now, for nearly two years, felt pleasantly familiar, a return of sorts to his home church, if he could be said to have one. Reverend Solshire fit the part well—a middle-aged man with a slight but sturdy body and the predictably pious voice, and his safe ecclesiastical jokes, suitable for a family audience. There was something slightly effeminate about him—his long, expressive fingers—and Daniel had wondered if he was "that way," like one of his assistants, but she told him he had four children and an adoring wife who always sat in the front row, staring reverently up at him. "Maybe it's all a front," he had suggested. "You never know with these ministers." She had elbowed him in the ribs.

They had met, of course, at work, that great incubator of romance, one balmy afternoon in late summer as she strolled leisurely back toward her workstation, as the warm wind pressed her light, flowing skirt into the shape of her legs, hair swirling around her face, and when he said hello she had been willing to stop and talk. There followed the usual escalation—lunches, walks, phone calls, a slow accretion of intimacies, each building to the next, a gradual coming together of hands and lips and body, punctuated by hesitations, doubts, regrets, but in the end the gravity of attraction, and their mutual loneliness was too powerful to be overcome or halted by common sense, or fears of how the drama would play out: the heart and body teaming up to trump the poor, straining brain, full of caution and would-be goodness.

That first day they met her head had tipped upward, as if to better receive the summer sun, and she was walking slowly, letting the wind have its way with her hair and skirt, as if she was looking, open to possibility, waiting for something to come to her. But that had been two and a half years before, and here she was now, in the pew beside him. Slight and pale, on a bad day she could look quite ordinary, but on a good one radiant and ebullient and joyful: she made him feel attractive, amusing, loved.

Little women with sharp elbows—that's who he was drawn to but not who he had married—an old story, often told. His wife, he had often been reminded, didn't have a mean bone in her body, was smart, wonderful, and kind. Everyone loved her, and sometimes suggested he treat her better. Why, he sometimes wondered, did he not feel guiltier than he actually did? When he had confessed his dual life once to a friend in a distant city, his friend had pondered it all and then said, gently, "But you're leaving something out. I haven't heard, in any of this, anything about Rebecca. What about her? Where does she fit in all this?" The simplicity of the question had hit him with a gentle, overwhelming weight that seemed to swell, with time, rather than diminish. He had found himself with no answer, at least not one he could come up with at the moment, and he was left to mull over this quiet but weighty rebuke, and the intimation that his undertaking, of which he was secretly proud, would generally be regarded as unspeakably selfish and cruel. But the mind had a wonderful ability to avoid, to *not* think about, that for which there was no palatable answer, or solution, or at least one he could entertain.

Solshire was warming to his topic, repeating lines of the lesson in his weighty tones, mellow and redolent with meaning, from Hebrews 10:17–22: *" 'I will remember their sins and their lawless deeds no more.' Where there is forgiveness of these, there is no longer any offering for sin. Therefore, my friends, since we have confidence to enter the sanctuary by the blood of Jesus, by the new and living way that he opened for us through the curtain (that is, through his flesh), and since we have a great priest over the house of God, let us approach with a true heart and full assurance of faith, with our hearts sprinkled clean from an evil conscience and our bodies washed with pure water."*

Sin—he had always been ill at ease with the concept, especially as expressed by the Catholics, as they seemed to think of little else, so that life became one long struggle against doing any of these awful things, doing them anyway, and then the weepy, weekly regret, penitence, confession, and request for forgiveness, always, apparently, granted. But what of goodness, and kindness, and of loving people? He could never make out much of this in the sermons. But as Solshire continued, he felt the old struggle rising up in him again, a desire to follow the thread of the sermon vying with his own rambling thoughts and wayward emotions, centered, as they had been for these more than two years now, on the woman sitting beside him, her eyes closed, her small pale hands folded onto themselves in her lap, her posture straight and true, the hat he had bought for her still on her head, purple suede. She had not called him early, as she often did, still in bed with her warm, sleepy voice, and when he had finally given up, caved in to his own impatience and called her, she had been cool, or at least busy, in the midst of her tussles with her daughter to get there on time.

"I'll see you in church," he had said, and then hung up without a proper good-bye. And yet, he felt good to be there, at peace, relieved from the chronic anxiety he often felt when they were apart. He closed his eyes and listened, her genuine reverence and belief trying to impart itself to him through layers of clothes. She had hopes for him—that his rather tepid interest in the church would bloom into something fuller, more complete, so that he and she could grow in faith, that the church would become a sanctuary for their love, a place where their relationship could be quietly admitted to—a hope for future happiness.

He stood and kneeled, and moved his lips, but his mind was elsewhere, bobbing along like a cork in a river. He was thinking of his own daughter, wrapped up in blankets with her doll, going to the kitchen for a bowl of cereal, back to the couch, laying the bowl on the floor where Daniel would find it, later, when he got home. There he would do a little work, tidy up the kitchen, help the girl with her homework, talk to his wife, and then, when the moment was right, when she skipped off down the street to play with a friend, and Rebecca settled into her study to do a little work for a presentation, and the cat curled up in the sunlight for a nap, he would steal away again, on some other vague pretext or other, into the car this time, for a drive south: 24.3 miles south, to be exact, thirty-five minutes with no traffic—first along the drive by the river, then onto the highway heading south—famously congested during the week but now, on the weekends, well traveled but moving—weaving its way down through the city in its series of bends and curves and familiar landmarks he knew by heart, turning off one high-way then onto another, then onto another smaller road, Route 26, once a country lane but now garishly cluttered in the usual American style—that particular brand of sprawl-ing ugliness that accrued before zoning laws: gas stations and ill-conceived malls, drugstores, a suntanning "spa," sev-eral flower shops, and then, toward the end, a tacky, cheap little amusement park featuring miniature golf and a haunted house—a jaunty wooden structure with hokey lettering and built at kooky angles that seemed to him unsafe. Fittingly, the body of a murder victim was once found stashed behind it. Somewhere along the road there was a hand-painted sign that said, in large letters, "Knives Sharpened," and he had often imagined visiting there, with his collection of dull saws and rusty knives: it would have given him a legitimate alibi, for once, but he had never managed to do it. It was the kind of place he generally, assiduously, avoided, and he was surprised to find himself there at all, waiting at the familiar lights, looking out at these improbable landmarks of which, in these two-plus years, he had become almost fond, as if his love for this woman had extended itself onto the very land-scape through which he had to pass to reach her.

These drives coincided with the rebroadcast of *A Prairie Home Companion*, another type of hokey Americana, and there was something about the combination—the passing landscape observed to the wholesome tonality of midwest-ern humor—that somehow leavened the true nature of his mission and its sordid associations: a married man traveling to visit his rather younger lover to spend the afternoon together—talk, eat, take a walk, watch sports on television, and, if the stars were in alignment, and the babysitter down the hall was available, or a good TV show was on, "com-plete" the day together, there on the bed that had become for him its own kind of sanctuary. Yet if Garrison Keillor was to be believed, all would turn out well, and whatever conflicts and hazards and guilt and blame there were to go around would be neatly wrapped up in a wave of chaste midwestern mirth, carried away on a country song, sung in the plaintive tones of a fading blond beauty in a cowboy hat.

Before him, high above him, in fact, in the pulpit that seemed to hang, suspended, from the wall, Solshire was talking about love, of all things, and how the love we felt for each other—our family, our friends, our husbands and wives, our children—was merely a manifestation, an expression, of God's love for us: more than that, it *was* God's love *for us,* flowing to us through another living soul, and we, somehow, were the conduits, the vehicles for this greater, all-encompassing emotion. There were not different *kinds* of love, the argument seemed to go, but just one great and universal love, of which all the others were fragments, diffractions, variations on a theme: would this not include, then, like a beam of sunlight through the colored glass, what he felt for the woman beside him, slight and mysterious and devout, moody and silent, then passionate and joyful, amused and appreciative of him in a way he had never felt before? Surely, God must recognize this love between them as genuine and pure and, circumstances aside, give them his blessing? She *did* love him, he was certain, and he felt loved by her, and if circumstances had been different, he had always known, he would have, well, ah well . . . No use dwelling on it now.

Fragments of biblical wisdom, remembered from his spotty religious training, floated up before him: "Judge not so ye shall not be judged." "Let he who has not sinned cast the first stone." And then, of Mary Magdalene, when the disciples were gathering their stones to pelt her with, "She has loved much, so much is forgiven her." He hoped the same could be said of him: he had loved much, so much would be forgiven him. Or did these aphorisms offer themselves only as convenient justifications, absolution, for his many and manifold sins—the adulterer's loophole?

"And then," Solshire continued, slowing down meaningfully, "there is that *other* kind of love, feelings of, and for, the flesh, feelings we share with our friends and neighbors from the animal kingdom, of which we, after all, are a part." A muffled wave of laughter passed across the great, vaulted spaces of the church. "What shall we make of these wants and desires? Where is the line between them, lust and love, bestial attraction and godly love, and who, after all, decides?" Like a breath of wind another wave of giddiness passed among the congregants, a few slouching adulterers perking up.

Daniel felt he knew whither all this was tending: physical desire within marriage was good and proper—a consummation between man and woman, an expression of God's own love for us—but outside of marriage was an abomination, more of the animal kingdom than the human. But what if this love was deep and all-consuming and complete? Which is more bestial, he would have liked to ask Reverend Solshire—the genuine passion and desire of two souls, *in love*, their bodies joined, as one, in something approaching the divine; or the world-weary lovemaking of a married couple, their mutual attraction long since dissipated in an endless procession of nights and days, duties and obligations, petty squabbles and the abrasions of domesticity and child rearing, the never-ending obligation of feeding oneself and others—a routine punctuated, now and then, by this almost primordial event, generally induced by too much red wine—a groping in the darkness toward another warm and living soul, a joining together, brief and elemental and surely more of the animal than the divine, less of love than habit, another need responded to, then afterward, the welcome and merciful return to oneself, and one's own part of the bed, and sleep?

But why to argue, now, with the sermon, with good man Solshire, to blaspheme in his mind, to take issue with this pleasant and comforting construction of love and church and family, and how each of us, more or less, could fit him- or herself into his tidy and comforting rubric: Could Daniel find, in this sturdy house of goodness, any place for himself? He could feel the gentle weight of these good people, with their righteous, uncomplicated lives, pressing up behind him, urging him on, impelling him toward the semicelestial platform of gold and candlelight, and a welcome taste of wine—his sacrament of every evening.

The sermon came to a close and Daniel, lost in his own ruminations, missed Solshire's somber, subtle denouement, ending not with a bang but a weighty, solemn whimper. They rose as one, and a hymn was sung by the nightingales: ... *"Then all shackles fall: the stormy clangour / of war's wild music in the earth shall cease; / love shall tread out the baleful fire of anger, / and in its ashes plant the tree of peace ... ,"* then the offering, a succession of kneels and stands and half-remembered blessings, then the long buildup into Communion.

But first there was the peace, turning to greet thy neighbor, and then to she who kissed him full on the lips, her lips soft and full and yielding, and when she said "Good morning," her eyes looked happy and open. "Nice to see you." And he knew that after the chilly confusions of the week he had been let back into her world, and his own heart unclenched itself, relaxed, and he felt he could breathe again.

"I see you brought your bag—going to do a little work in church, are you?" she added, smiling, a friendly barb at his alibi. He would let it pass and add it to his collection.

He shook another couple of hands behind him—a

tweedy Brahmin and his wife, a fierce-looking beauty with a very firm handshake and pale blue eyes, the color of an iceberg as seen from below. All that talk about love had stirred him up, and even now, his efforts at piety were under pressure from other thoughts, incursions of the erotic and aspirations for what, later that afternoon, might transpire between them—thoughts ill fitting to a church, and yet enhanced by it, "pleasures of the flesh" of which, after all, everyone present here in the sanctuary, even Solshire himself, was a consequence, intended or otherwise. What if, he had sometimes wondered, you could somehow preserve each of these individual moments of consummation, collapsed by time and gathered together here in the sanctuary, and release them as sound, a single chorus—a great and magnificent song rising up and swirling in the high vaulted spaces of the church, falling back and then gathering force in a final, glorious crescendo—truly, a "joyful noise" made unto the Lord. He smiled inwardly, and would have liked to share his aural vision, but would have to keep it to himself: she didn't like church jokes.

Later that day, perhaps, they would act out their own private drama, as the weak afternoon light filtered through the window, and her weary daughter settled into a television stupor in the adjoining room, and the Sunday meal they had just eaten settled within them, and he quickly washed the dishes, part of their ritual, and the two of them, woozy and amorous, would steal away to her room, close the door, and make love with a tender passion that surely transcended the "merely physical." And as she lay in his arms, her slight, pale body held against his, time would catch up with them, as the light faded outside, and the swaying shadows of spring leaves were cast from a streetlight on the wall of her room, and her daughter (alas, too late!!) clamored against the locked door to get in, and he would have to get ready to leave. And then, from across town, the mournful bellow of the departing train, the 5:03—once, twice, three times—and that's when the pain of circumstance would rise up again as she drifted off to sleep in his arms, her body so slight he could sometimes not tell if she was there in the bed at all. He hated it, this leave-taking, so quiet yet abrupt and somehow violent, abandoning her in the bed alone, his own needs fulfilled, and what should have been the quiet resolution of the day together cut off, ended prematurely. He would kiss her then, murmur good-bye, thank her for a lovely afternoon, and steal away—down the hall to the elevator, slowly descending to the street, and then breaking into a half run to his car and in, just as the bells from a nearby church chimed and rolled over the sleepy town—the second parenthesis to their day. He would call home from the car to announce he was on his way, hoping for the answering machine, his alibi losing traction.

His drive took place in the darkness of winter, the twilight of spring, or the still bright light of a summer evening. On the radio there was another show he generally listened to, which turned, with twilight, into jazz, with another mellow-toned host, and as he swiftly passed through back roads that led back to Route 26, it was with a palpable calmness, filled up with her, sated with food, and company and love, the taste of her still on his lips, a fullness of body and spirit tarnished, only, by the bittersweet moment of departure, as she lay, drowsing still in the bed, naked under the covers, and he kissed her cheek and stole away—a small act of violence, this loving her, then leaving. "The timekeeper," she sometimes called him, both fondly and with an edge of one who had been left too often, and too soon. What if, just once, he did not leave, did not go home as planned, but stayed out all night as others did, showed up the next day, without explanation? Not possible. There was, too, the great unspoken possibility—plan B—that he could leave his life, wife and daughter, study and cat, woodpile and the grass he had just planted in the backyard, the new couch they had bought, the pleasant life on a tree-lined street in the city, not far from the job where he worked. A wife, perhaps, was one thing, a grown woman with her own career; but how do you leave a child, your own flesh and blood, the only one you will have in this life, to go and live with another, different child, one who doesn't even really like you?

Instead, he would drive swiftly home and arrive back into the city to the sound track of Count Basie or Thelonious Monk, and slip back into his life within the window of plausibility, unsuspected—or at least not remarked upon. Women, the talk shows assure us, always know, and choose not speak, to break the peace with questions whose answers they may not want to hear. By the time he would call Rachel later, call back to the place he had just come from, she would be asleep, or would have turned the phone off, and his low-grade anxieties would slowly return, a need to see her, to reconnect, to assure himself that all was still well between them.

Unlike the Episcopalian church of his long lost summers, which offered Communion only on the first Sunday of the month, this one reenacted the ritual every week, at least at the nine o'clock service, and it was always awkward, the buildup, and gathering question of whether, finally, he should participate: in truth he never had taken Communion, was a virgin of the altar, felt it was something of a lie to stand there, take the wine and wafer as if he really believed and was taking in the body and blood of Christ in earnest. And so he would remain, as she and her daughter pressed out past him and then returned, waiting for the hour to wind itself out. It always took longer than he expected.

She let go of his hand and returned it to her own lap, and he was alone again in the pew, connected to no part of her physical being. He wondered, sometimes, how he fit in all this—into her devotion to church, to God—but knew that she did not see it as a contradiction or conflict, but rather the opposite, a way of bringing him into her life, suggesting a possible resolution: yet it was *she* he wanted to be closer to, and if the church could help, who was he to object? Or perhaps conversely, it was his love of her that had brought him finally into the fold of the church—the lost sheep, found in the wilderness, and brought in by the lovely shepherd beside him? People stood:

> *The Lord be with you.*
> And also with you.
> *Lift up your hearts.*
> We lift them to the Lord.
> *Let us give thanks to the Lord our God.*
> It is right to give God thanks and praise.
> *It is right and a good and joyful thing.*
> *Always and everywhere to give thanks to you,*
> Father Almighty Creator of Heaven and Earth.

In this, at least, he believed: it was right to give thanks to the creator of heaven and earth and the firmament, and all the creatures who moved upon it—one must be grateful for this strange miracle of life which, after all, need not have been, could have been otherwise—we did not *need* to be—one could have never existed, and one day wouldn't, except in the hearts and minds and memory of those who loved us, but then even this, with their own deaths, would be taken away.

"*But chiefly we are bound to praise you for the glorious resurrection of your son Jesus Christ our Lord; for he is the true Paschal lamb, who was sacrificed for us, and has taken away the sins of the world. By his death he has destroyed death, and by his rising to life again he has won for us everlasting life.*"

Here was another fork in the road he would come to, a

shadowy thicket in the forest—the promise of eternal life for all the believers, for those with faith; and for those without, or with not enough, back to dust, to the elements, to be blown about in the barren desert among the rocks and the bones of beasts and men, to be forgotten. But what became of us, our flesh and blood? Where to spend *forever* if not in our own earthly vessels, our own friendly bodies, which have given us so much pain and pleasure along the way?

And what of "faith"? In the existence of God? Faith that all of these stories were true, that the miracles actually happened, that Jesus was actually crucified, buried, then rose from the dead as described in Scripture? Faith that, at the end of the day, when one died, a decision would actually be made of your life on earth, "judgment," you would ascend to heaven or, conversely, plunge into hell, and thereafter spend eternity? This seemed a little severe, and this is where he drew the line, where his belief ground to a halt in the sand, and he peered over the edge of a precipice into nothingness—a world without him. It was this that somehow terrified him: not only the death of himself, but also of all who had known and loved him—the death of an entire family, one by one and over time, so that even the constellation of love that had held them together, with its strong and fragile bonds, would be lost forever. At such moments of clarity he could actually cry out, sit up in a bed at the quiet horror of it all, or shake the thought away as he walked down some sunlit street on a beautiful summer day, trying to purge from his mind thoughts of eternal nothingness, nonexistence, and try to concentrate, instead, on the present—on the swaying checkered skirt of the young woman walking a few dozen yards ahead, the shape of her as perceived from a distance, his own quickening step behind her.

When they all settled back into their seats, the child, Amelia, returned from her Sunday-school class, came down the aisle to the pew, pushed past his knees, and then pressed, rather pointedly, down into the nonexistent space between himself and her mother, forcing them apart. He was tempted to give her the old finger-to-the-ribs treatment, but decided against it, as it might set off a chain of events beyond his control— whining and retaliation, and a mother who would blame him for the skirmish.

Then there was a strange *"Holy, holy,"* a kind of chanted and long-winded incantation leading into Communion— *"Whenever you drink it, do so in remembrance of me"*—and then the only part of the service he knew by heart, the Lord's Prayer: when it came around he joined in ardently, as it evoked a happy memory of childhood—his own father kneeling beside the bed, and then, together, them running through the words like a mountain stream running over the smooth, worn stones, their voices joined in a kind of harmony: " ... *forgive us our trespasses, as we forgive those who trespass against us, and lead us not into temptation, but deliver us from evil, for thine is the Kingdom, the power, and the glory, forever and ever, Amen."* For a time he had continued the practice with his daughter, Jennie, but then, for reasons not entirely clear to him—laziness, lack of conviction, his own ongoing distractions—it had petered out: something else to feel guilty for.

The Communion began in silence—the ushers first, and then a procession of robed choristers filed down along the sides of the church, singing the whole while an infectious low-grade hymn, and then back up together along the center aisle, upward onto the altar, where they circled around and behind and received the wine and the host before returning to the choir. Unlike other churches he had been to, this one processed back to front, so as they sat he could feel the slow wave of the devoted approaching from behind. He had grown fond of the ritual, the predictable orderliness of it, and enjoyed, even, the moment of separation when the usher appeared beside them, took one step backward, and held out his hand in invitation; mother and daughter finally stood, and left him there alone in the pew. But as they waited for the usher to reach them, the child beside him, forgetting for a moment that they were not the best of friends, stood up, leaned against his knee, and then, in the silent language of children, raised her arms to convey a desire to be picked up and pulled onto his lap, and he, both reluctant and touched, obliged, hoisted her up onto his knees. So light and fine, this child, with the bones of a bird, so unlike the heft of his own daughter, who had inherited her mother's strength and size and bones. He let his arms surround her, and he pulled her toward him, paternally and gently, this child who had come into his life through no fault of her own, her own father having fled at the first word of conception and disappeared forever. But the modest weight of her on his lap, and the hymn the chorus was singing, filling the church with its otherworldliness, and the sparks of candles on the altar, and the weight of the woman beside him, so laden with love and desire and confusion, and then the thought and image of Jennie, his own flesh and blood, alone on the sofa watching her inane cartoons, unsupervised, and his wife upstairs in the bed, in the house he had abandoned for these stolen hours, induced in him an undesired response inside his head, a tickling behind his nose, somewhere, and then he observed, with a kind of helpless regret, that his eyes had filled up with tears. In the middle distance the lights of the candles diffracted into a kind of starry, salty prism, and he attempted to discreetly wipe away his tears with the back of his hand before anyone noticed, but the child, ever vigilant and sensing there had been a sea change beneath her, looked around, stared, then tugged at her mother's shirtsleeve and whispered, loudly, "He's crying, Mommy, look!" She didn't look, but continued to stare ahead, deep in her devotions, and with a raised finger told her to hush.

He had wept before in church, for no good reason—moved by the spectacle and his own helplessness in the face of circumstance, the knowledge that there was no remedy, that he would have to ride it out to some natural, or unnatural, conclusion, with either a bang or a whimper. But now the tears would not stop: the girl on the couch; he, here in the church with a different child on his lap and another woman beside him; and he, the interchangeable part, the apex of two triangles between which he scurried back and forth, trying to keep the precarious geometry of both intact, lest his fragile house of cards—her analogy—come tumbling down. He was in the middle, the cause of it all, "the architect of disaster"—his metaphor. But he could no more leave Rachel, he knew, than he could leave his own wife and daughter—the only child, he suspected, he would ever have.

Impelled by gravity, the tears were now running down his cheek, and the child kept looking up to see if he could get it together, so the next time she glanced at him he gave her his own squinchy mouse face to get her to stop.

"Leave it at the foot of the cross," Rachel had sometimes said, for problems one could not solve, for which there was no apparent solution. *Pray*, in short, and so he had tried, with moderate success, but it was a comfort he felt he did not fully deserve.

He could feel, now, the wave of Communion takers growing closer, the line gathering beside him, and then the usher was right beside him, his papery hands reverently clasped, and then he took one step backward and extended his arm, inviting them to rise; the child quickly slid off his knee, Rachel stood beside him, and when she offered her hand he took it, rose with them, and joined them in their slow procession toward the altar, inching forward with the other congregants.

Distracted by physical activity, he noticed that his tears had stopped, and he tidied up his face and they advanced, one step at a time, then turned and stepped up a short flight of velvet steps into the greater brightness of the altar. There the lost sheep were slowly moving, like the inner workings of a celestial clock, waiting, then kneeling in turn, then rising and filing back to their pews.

The sound of the chorus filled the space with a low, melodious keening, and as they gathered around, his own hands clasped now, he was aware of being highly visible there, exposed, next to Rachel and the child, together in this sacred space, but who could criticize a man preparing to accept the blood and body of Christ into his own, fallible being? To their left the parishioners waited in turn; then, at the silent invitation of an usher, they moved down into a space for three, the child beside him. They knelt; he held his hands cupped together, as others had done, waiting to receive the host. Lightning did not strike him, as he half expected, nor was he cast away by some divine intervention, as a skeptic or a half believer, nor did he experience any great light of revelation coming into his body, filling him up. What he felt, rather, was a pleasant and powerful mélange of sensual impressions—the warmth of the place, the soft white light of stone all around, glowing, as if lit from within, the scent of incense and smoke of candles, and people before him, like intermediaries to some other world, white robed and close, and silent, save for the faint rustling of the cloth. He was conscious too of kneeling beside her, with her, surrounded by people he did not know, yet who were witnesses of a kind. Before him, the white robes were moving back and forth like angels, and to his right, murmured invitations growing closer, *"body of Christ . . . blood of . . . ,"* then the glow of silver holding the bread, and then a piece of bread, pleasantly rough, torn from a larger one, was pressed down into his palms. It was Solshire himself and, true to his impressions, his hands *were* small, and slightly effeminate. He took the bread into his mouth and without warning the silver bowl appeared at his lips, holding the deep-ruby-colored liquid, tipped toward him, into him, not just a taste, a full mouthful—"*blood of Christ,*" Solshire said, wiping the chalice as he moved away.

He let the wine meet and mingle with the bread, closed his eyes for a moment, and then stood up, making space as the child exhorted, "Come on, Daniel!" She raced ahead with her mother and he followed, aware that he still held the wine and bread in his mouth, savoring the taste, before he finally swallowed and left the altar. He followed them down the stairs and returned to the darkened spaces of the church, relieved, and sat back down in the cushioned pew where he belonged.

"You didn't do it right!" the child whispered fiercely beside him, scolding, but he didn't answer. He continued to stare straight ahead, back into the candlelight and swirling smoke where figures were still moving, as in a dream. And from somewhere came to him the small epiphany he had been waiting for, lines of a poem that had been lost, hidden in folds of memory from his long lost, once hopeful, youth. The title and the author's name had been forgotten, but the words had stayed with him all these years. "What gifts there are," the poet had written, "are all here, in this world."

Old Girlfriends

"Do you still love her?" Sonya wanted to know, listing slightly forward in her chair, pausing, then sinking back as she watched him squirm under the solemn weight of her question. He looked out the window for an answer, and found instead a few yellow leaves that seemed to have remembered it was almost fall. She was speaking of Marianne, his old college girlfriend, who had led him to Sonya in the first place, and who sat in the same green velvety chair on Thursdays, two to three, he believed, and spilled out her own litany of confusions and grievances against the world—himself among them.

"I think so," he said, with usual indecisiveness, fully aware that the answer would not pass muster. "Yes, I still love her," he added, firmly, shifting, sitting up. "But I don't know if we could ever, you know, get back together."

"Exactly!" she said, and fixed him in the deep black pools of her eyes, with what he hoped was a soft glow of approval. Unlike most therapists, Sonya was not afraid to let you know if you had gotten the wrong or right answer.

Her slight smile suggested Mona Lisa. Her lips were painted a deep ruby red, and her dark hair rose with a kind of airy weightlessness above her head. Her bosom, compressed yet full, heaved. Her arms lay on the desk between them, and on one of them, the left, was a row of blue numbers, somewhat imperfectly drawn, as if by a child just learning to write or an adult using an imperfect tool: a crude tattoo penned in the hand of an SS officer, weary, perhaps, from scrawling countless such numbers on the forearms of all those being admitted to Buchenwald, or Auschwitz, as Sonya had been as a fetching fifteen-year-old with deep, dark eyes, in 1941.

"Trevor," she finally said, in the tone of summary, welcome hint that the end of the hour was mercifully approaching. "We have a lot of work to do." He wanted to ask her what kind of work, what was still wrong with him, but he knew what she would say, happily: "Everything!" He wanted to make a final reach for the pack of cigarettes that lay on her desk, halfway between them, but that would have been his third—one over his unspoken quota. Instead, he put his hands on the green velour arms of the chair, ready for liftoff, and she said in her thick accent, Polish, "Next week, same time, same station?"

"Yes, thank you." He pushed the small white envelope that held his, now her, fifty dollars. They stood up simultaneously, revealing an unimportant truth: Sonya was not tall—short, in fact—as stolid as a fire hydrant. He took the tray and coffee cup, opened the door, and let himself out, and as he descended the plush carpeting she shouted down from the top of the stairs, "Annie, please! More poison! Alphonse, come up. Trevor—good-bye, and remember— homework!!"

"I will," he said, knowing full well what his homework was—thinking about himself. At the bottom of the stairs he said hello to Alphonse, a dapper, smooth-skinned man giving off a fragrance of cleanliness and cologne, wearing a shiny blue cravat—a gay monk, he happened to know. Sonya was not very good at confidentiality.

A soft gray light filtered through the curtains into the neatly cluttered room, full of books and baubles, casting it in a soft funereal gloom. He had hoped to filch a final cigarette from a pack that often lay on a small glass table near the corner, but was aware of Annie's soft, shuffling presence behind him. He took the tray into the kitchen and set it down on the counter.

"All right, darling. Thank you," she said in her liquid southern drawl. "You have yourself a good week." She was a tall, slender woman from Alabama, slightly stooped, but with a youngish, pretty face of nut brown skin, lightly laced with freckles. It sometimes seemed to him that he made this journey to Sonya's less to have his head examined than to be asked, upon arrival, if he wanted some coffee and "a couple of cookies," and be called "darling" in Annie's mild, mellifluous voice. Hers was a soft, nurturing presence, gentle and kind, as opposed to Sonya's robust urgency—like a giraffe and a lion living together in a small tidy house on the edge of the forest.

"Good-bye, darling," Annie said, letting him out into the gray light. The door clicked shut behind him.

It was always a relief to be outside again, the taste of coffee and cigarettes on his tongue.

His car, recently acquired, was an eight-year-old VW Beetle of a metallic, faded blue, and sat by the curb like a cat. He was fond of it but wary, for in his first month of ownership it had already proven troublesome, had refused to start several times and left him stranded in inconvenient places, like southbound on the Henry Hudson Parkway, or on Eighty-sixth during rush hour. And there was always a tinge of anxiety when he was about to turn the key, a gathering apprehension that it would refuse to start, but it did so now with a lusty little growl of affirmation, the sound of a World War I biplane, sending a plume of blue smoke out the back; he was off and away, bouncing through the bumpy streets of Queens and onto the perilous web of parkways and thruways that would eventually take him back to his new home.

The urban sprawl around him was ugly, of course, but there was a kind of wonderful New York beauty to it all— the winding, uneven highway, the trucks and cars zooming past him on either side, burned-out husks of cars left by the side of the road where they had been picked clean then torched by urban vultures, various billboards and land-marks, like the giant sign that said "Tastee." And to his left, looming over the landscape, the enormous metal globe from the World's Fair grounds he had attended as a child almost twenty years before, his hot and tired family traipsing across an endless parking lot to visit the wonders of the coming world: 1965.

Ahead, he could see the towers of the Throg's Neck Bridge rising before him like the gates to Oz, and he was careful not to miss his exit and be flung out into the wilder-ness of Long Island, like a space capsule thrown into outer orbit: instead, he made the sharp turn at the exit and rose up the antiquated bridge, strangely narrow and steep and parabolic, hurtling down again into the southern edge of Westchester—past Co-op City and a murky salt marsh or two, west on the Cross County Parkway, right, up and around and over Yonkers, and he was home free, decelerating into the relative safety of the cozy river towns, his own among them: two small rooms in the back of a large baronial house that sat in the leafy suburbs, overlooking the broad, shimmering back of the Hudson.

Back to school! This, too, had been Sonya's idea. During their first or second session the previous winter, she had conducted a short, practical interview, asked him what, as a child, he had thought he would do when he was older, and after only a few short minutes declared, "I think you should go to graduate school, for teaching," an idea which, truth be told, had never occurred to him. But he had been doing some substitute teaching already, he told her, at which she beamed. "I think you would be a wooonderful teacher," she said, in her low, resonant voice, seasoned by nicotine. "But first you must get a degree!"

And with a new lightness and sense of purpose he had applied, cajoled his college transcript out of the registrar's office of his alma mater, Brown, and been accepted. Thrice a week thereafter he would steer his new car south, down the winding Saw Mill, over the Harlem River at Spuyten Duyvil, then along the Henry Hudson Parkway to Ninety-sixth, north on Riverside with his eagle eye out for parking spots, artfully backed into before trudging over to the Teachers College, a homely, northern adjunct to Columbia.

His fellow students were a curious mélange, none of whom, it seemed at first glance, would offer respite from his life of chastity and solitude—the first time he had been girlfriendless since his junior year of college. Within a couple weeks, he had fallen in with a bunch of like-minded types—back-of-the-classroom wisenheimers who would make comical remarks to each other and, after Friday-night class, would generally repair to a local tavern on Broadway for a beer. Sydney, a foppish throwback to the forties, always in a suit and necktie, horn-rimmed glasses, well-combed hair with a perfect part held in place with some gelling agent; Joey, Birkenstocked and bearded, wide-eyed and affable, from California; and Greg, sharp-witted, left-leaning Jew, newly minted from one of those frosty, semi-elite Maine colleges—Colby or Bates or Bowdoin—who was going into teaching as a means for spreading the word of social justice and indoctrinating vulnerable students to his parboiled

Marxist rhetoric. There were some young women who came along too, sometimes, of median levels of allure, none of whom, quite, to borrow Sydney's sardonic phrase, "rocked his boat."

During the first week of class they had been "invited" to introduce themselves, and among their fellow students had been a short pretty woman with soft, expressive eyes. Everyone else had stayed in their seats, slouching in a mixture of diffidence and laziness, but she had stood up and spoken in that soft, lilting voice. "My name is Daya Masunda, and I am from Harare, the capital of my native country, Zimbabwe." She was wearing white boots and beige corduroy pants, and as she spoke, her two hands were holding each other lightly, for company. She had full, pretty lips, perfectly defined like those etched in ancient stone on the friezes of Egyptian tombs he had studied in college. "I am here pursuing my doctorate in international education, and I would be very happy to meet any of you, after class, sometime." Her voice was soft but perfectly clear, each word making a pleasant shape in the stale air. Her white boots were shyly padding the floor, like someone walking in place. She paused, and then said, "Thank you." The class lightly applauded at the earnestness and clarity of her introduction. He was going to make good on her offer, but by the end of class, as he rose from his seat, he saw her slip out the door and she was gone.

In any case, he had made a minor pact with himself to remain single, girlfriendless, for an entire year, dating from the late-winter dissolution of his previous relationship with Alexis, a tumultuous and beautiful Italian with whom he had spent a couple of jumbled postcollegiate years, alternating doses of pleasure and pain (the three *f*'s, as one of his friends put it—fighting, feuding, and fucking)—swiftly moving cycles of dramatic discord and euphoric reconciliation. He was eager to avoid such wearying drama in his next romance. He had already made it for seven months of partial chastity, aside from a short tryst with a rabbi's daughter he had met one afternoon at a church fair looking over the wicker baskets; like him, she had plenty of spare time on her hands, but in the mornings she liked to lie in bed for hours, trying to lure him back in. He was too much of a New Englander for that, and with time she had drifted away.

And then one October afternoon on his way back from Sonya's, he had heard a beep, beep, beeping beside him, and was about to flip someone the bird when he looked over to the beaming face of Marianne. She pointed to the side of the road, and they pulled over into an abandoned gas station where the SUNOCO letters, long since removed, had left their ghostly shadow in the dust. As he approached her she smiled and laughed, gave him a long hug, reminding him of how well their bodies had once fit together. But she seemed smaller than he remembered, and her hair was slightly redder, and finer; she was wearing glasses now, and was looking less like the Gypsy palm reader he once knew than a housewife, or a law student, which she was. "Well, fancy meeting you here!"

"Fresh from our mutual head doctor—your friend Sonya, and her cigarettes."

"No kidding!" she said. "You're still at it?"

"Sure. I'm not yet cured, as she likes to remind me." She was living farther north, up the same mighty river, while going to school and working as a legal aid in Queens, keeping company with murderers and rapists and drug dealers arguing their innocence. He had imagined for a time, earlier that fall, that they might suddenly get back together, a joyful and inevitable reunion, but could now feel, as she stood beside him, this would never happen. In college, she had worn a Tibetan hat and read palms and the I Ching in a downtown Providence park by the canal, and she wrote her thesis on the Dalai Lama—even met him once, when he came to talk. Only later did she decide to become a lawyer; she returned to school, and started to fall in love with candidates even more hopeless than he had been—a foppish, Frisbee-throwing undergraduate, and now, from India, some guy named "Mister" who was already betrothed to someone back in Bombay. (Like Alexis, she liked to confide details of her private life, hurts and needs and wants, as if, having failed in their own romance, he could now serve as romantic adviser.) After college, they had lived together for almost a year in a house shared with five others, slept on a single bed on a parquet floor, and not once, as far as he could remember, made love. How had he done this? When he asked her "Why?" she seemed sad and helpless, and said, "I don't know."

She had loved him once, but he had squandered it, or not fully reciprocated, and by the time he joined her in New York it was too late to rebuild the campfire, to restart the fading embers, to get the genie back into the bottle. One thing he had figured out about women: once a door was closed, it seldom reopened; nonetheless, as they stood together in the shadow of the long-abandoned station, he was aware that they were holding hands.

"And what about you—it's great that you've gone back to school," she was saying, in the russet, orangey light. "You'll be a wonderful teacher!" Why did everyone think this? Because he couldn't do anything else? "Do you like it?"

"Not bad. Better than working in the bookstore, like last year. It was Sonya's idea—I do everything she says, so she doesn't get mad. Plus, there's a teacher shortage, and they promise they'll find us a job."

"In the city?"

"Maybe—or maybe I'll head north, closer to my family. Maybe I'm not a city mouse after all, or I'm a smaller-city mouse—Hartford or New Haven. Closer to the country." It was true. Lately he felt himself listing back toward the woods and fields of his New England roots. She invited him to a family party a few weeks away, and he accepted. It would be good to see her parents again, the curly-haired genius brothers he used to get high with in their Long Island backyard, some of her pretty younger sisters he not so secretly admired. He gave her a long hug, familial in tone, packed her back into her car, and watched her head north on the Saw Mill. He felt no pang of nostalgia or regret, and he made a note to tell Sonya: she would be proud of him. His car, never turned off, was still growling and patiently spluttering, waiting to be taken home.

The previous spring he had been living in Brooklyn, traveled to Sonya's by subway, followed by a fifteen-minute walk through the tidy neighborhood in Queens; afterward he would retrace his steps to the subway, where his return voyage happily coincided with the dismissal of a large local high school. As he sat the train would fill up with these perfumed beauties to keep him company for the long ride home, and as he sat, or stood, or read his book, as the lights of the trains flickered on and off and they sped through the tunnel, he would study these girls who had suddenly surrounded him at a surprising and wonderful proximity: so beautiful, he found them, the Asians in their shy and whispering packs, the Latinas with their tight jeans and bright lipstick and their belly buttons looking boldly out at the world like a third eye, the bawdy Americans, both beige and brown, their beckoning, knowing bodies cloaked in improbable styles of high school chic, their wide eyes and cackling laughs and scissoring, masticating, gum-chewing mouths so different from the pale, restrained beauties of his own chaste Connecticut town.

"You sexualize women!" Sonya had accused him once, but, he wanted to retort, they had been sexualized already, by their maker—and he was merely the helpless onlooker, powerless before their beauty and his desire. And how, he wondered as he gazed upward at the melancholy face of the girl across the aisle, her soft brown eyes staring languidly past him, her full pretty lips the color of the rose, could he deny or pretend that she was not among the most beautiful women in the world? And how to deny that everywhere he went in this great, lonely city he saw—on the subway, in the street, trapped in the glass booth of the token seller's window—women who filled him with a longing that he, shy by nature and uneager to offend, felt powerless to act upon, or express. Among the courses he wished they had offered in college would have been "How to Talk to Attractive Strangers," along with "What to Do with the Rest of Your Life" and "The Practical Applications of a Liberal Arts Education—If Any!"

By the time he reached Brooklyn and came up again into daylight, he was exhausted from himself, and from the cigarettes, coffee, and confessional hangover he had from his session with Sonya. Emerging from the romantic kingdom of the subway he would drift slowly back toward his street, his rented room, in the large apartment of a Jewish divorcée and her daughter, a gloomy young woman (her virginity, he suspected, still festering within her) who spent most of her time in her room alone, dressed in black, listening to the records whose sad strains he could hear, muffled, through the walls.

It wasn't until late October that he first made contact with his classmate from Zimbabwe, whose name he had forgotten but, after a frantic search, found scrawled in his notebook as part of his irreverent commentary on their lecture. "Daya Masunda—Zimbabwe . . . pretty voice, eyes, lips . . . feet tapping the floor . . . white boots . . ." After several failures at catching her after class, he had revised his strategy, avoided his usual seat in the back, loitered in the hallway reading and rereading a single billboard; when he caught her coming into class he said hello, clumsily followed her to a seat two from her own. During the break he leaned over and asked her how she liked the class and city; he'd like to learn something about Zimbabwe, too, he remarked stupidly, at which point she grew a little curt, bit her lip, and said, "That's easy—there are lots of books about it—it's public information, there for those who really want it. You don't need me for that."

"Good idea," he said, raising a single finger in the air, conceding her unexpected point, making a slight bow of regret; but, not wanting to lose his focus, he added, "And maybe next week you'll join us for a beer? There's a bunch of us who go across the street, to the Broadway Tavern, after class."

"All right, maybe," she said. "When my job is over. Then maybe I can learn something about this big, strange country of yours, too." Touché! He smiled at the rejoinder, shook her hand for the second time (strong and firm). They parted amicably, but he could see he would need to proceed gingerly. Nonetheless, to his surprise, as he sat over his second beer the following Friday, doing imitations of their least favorite teacher, Lori Mortner, who had hair like a spaniel's and whose lectures were punctuated with references to her colleagues as "a giant in his field" ("Yes—a field of mice," Sydney would whisper), he saw her through several panes of glass approach the bar and look tentatively in; he got up and went to the door.

"You're still here," she said. "Oh, all right. I just got off work. I wasn't sure if you'd still be here or not." A chair was found and she settled in between Sydney and bearded Joey, who immediately started in with his well-intentioned questions about her country, his head held at a sympathetic tilt, nodding sagely, plucking his beard. She fielded them politely, but it wasn't until Joey had left and she ordered her second glass of white wine that she quietly complained, "Goodness, people here are so direct. So many questions. At home, I guess, we find things out more slowly. . . . They don't bombard you all at once."

"But wouldn't you rather just be asked, and get it out of the way?" Sydney offered. "Then you know where you all stand?" He had a slow, deliberate way of speaking, like the characters in old fifties movies in their suits and gray fedoras.

"I know where *I* stand already," she rejoined, then softened. "Maybe later, but not the first time."

"I see," he said, rubbing his chin. Penny, an almost pretty blonde from Seattle, was sitting beside him, and there seemed to be some romantic possibility brewing. "People in the West are like that too. They might just say, 'How are you doing today?' and take it from there."

"I think that's better," Daya said. Her soft, pretty eyes reflected as sparks the warm candlelight of the Broadway Tavern, and she had taken out her braids in favor of a short Afro that Trevor was dying to get his hands into. Sydney was getting his itchy, gotta-go look, studied the bill quizzically, rubbing his own thighs, and then gathered a crumpled sheaf of notes on the table. "That should cover us, myself, and young Penny here—just a lime soda, right? Two vodka martinis for me. A pleasure to meet you," he said, rising and shaking her hand theatrically. "And I will see you later, sport." Left alone, he fought off the impulse to have a fourth beer, and watched Daya finish her wine.

"He's interesting," she offered of Sydney.

"Odd, you might say. He's like a character out of a fifties movie. 'Sport'?—nobody talks like that anymore."

When it was time to go she reached into her wallet, but he waved her off. Though cheap by nature, he had learned some old-world chivalry from Sonya: "You must pay for the woman!" he remembered her growling. "Of course!! I don't care what the feminists say: women want a man who can take care of them! They can be liberated afterward—in the bedroom!"

He walked her a block to her dorm, admired the warmth and loveliness of the evening, the slopes and curves of the nut-brown skin that demurely descended down into her dress.

"Oh well, thank you for inviting me."

"You're welcome." He gave her a half hug in parting, did not try to kiss her, and made his way to the car, a new lightness about him, autumnal sense of possibility.

And then one Saturday morning he was introduced, in the town's only bookstore, to a woman a couple years younger than he, fresh from some fancy liberal arts college—a short, bubbling girl from the Midwest who was working nearby in some sort of think tank, mulling over ethical issues related to medicine. She was living on Main Street, across from a bar; one Friday night they had a few drinks, and later she showed him her apartment, introduced him to her two circling cats. The rooms were dark and carpeted, and gave off the fragrance of too many cleansers, and the cats were eyeing him warily, but despite his impression that he could make himself comfortable, that she would not mind if he stayed, he kissed her on the cheek, took note of the pleasant warm imprint of her body against his, and went home. Better to preserve the possibility than push his luck and bollix the whole thing up. Romantic opportunity traveled in twos or threes, it seemed, like meteor showers.

At the end of October, earnest, radical Greg hosted a Halloween party at his apartment somewhere in the lower hundreds: a modest affair with beer and some tacos that kept emerging from his ancient oven, a few people dressed in halfhearted costumes. By prearrangement he had met Daya outside her dorm, and walked her down the dozen blocks to the apartment, then up to the fourth floor. Sydney was there, dressed as himself, only more so, a dandy of the 1920s, and pretty Penny in a black spandex suit, with whiskers on her cheeks. But mostly it was margaritas, and a tub of cheap beer, and gloomy seventies music on his stereo. Whenever he came into a room, change-the-world Greg, with his head full of dark Mediterranean curls, seemed to be hovering over Daya, talking politics and social change, demonstrating an effortful knowledge of Africa and its postcolonial travails, and Trevor felt a twinge of something, the primal recognition of a rival. She was wearing the same white boots, and tighter pants, a V-neck sweater that revealed the same cleavage that had been haunting his imagination of late.

By chance, he had given a ride to bouncy Alice that night to attend a party of her own, and had foolishly agreed to give her a ride home as well, at a certain time and corner, an obligation he now regretted. Nonetheless, he was dutiful if nothing else, could not abandon her, and as the hour approached he told Daya he had to leave, and offered her a ride back to her dorm. She was sparring with Greg at the time, but as host he was not free to depart, and Trevor took a certain pleasure in terminating their discussion. Outside, as they walked to the car, their pace slowed to a saunter in harmony with the warm late-October night; a silvery moon was ascending in the east, visible down the canyon of each crosstown street, inviting them to pause at each intersection. They found his car first, and he drove slowly, discussing each of their classmates; then they were there, at her dorm. "That was fun," she said, and he reached over and offered his hand, palm up. She took it in hers, but then looked away, out the window, and said, "Gosh."

"What?"

"Oh, nothing, just in my culture, we are not so direct." Her hand was warm and strong and she did not let go.

"Well, I'll see you in class." Her thumb was giving the back of his hand a small massage. "I'd better go," she said, but still continued to sit, then added, "Do you want to come in?"

Now it was his turn to be surprised. "I would, but I told a friend I would give him a ride back to Westchester—I have to pick him up down on Ninety-sixth Street." The lie had come instinctively, without forethought or planning.

"Oh, all right," she said, still looking out the window. "Then I'll see you in class, I guess. Call me if you wish— extension 347, Granger Hall."

"Three forty-seven," he repeated, and then watched her as she went up the steps, turned the key, waved, and went into her dorm.

He swore to himself in parting, sped and sputtered down to Ninety-sixth Street, where Alice was waiting in a pool of yellow light the same color of her hair—a beacon to would-be muggers. "I thought you might have gotten lucky and ditched me," she said with a chuckle.

"No, I gave someone a ride back to her dorm after the party." On the drive home they compared notes: she laughed a lot, and appeared to be even drunker than he. When he pulled up in front of her door she slapped and searched and rummaged through her bag frantically, with the inevitable conclusion: she had forgotten her keys!! A moment of panic! Too late to call the landlord—she didn't even have his number. "He opens the deli at seven a.m. I can catch him then," she said, failing to mention that that was seven hours into the future.

He knew his lines: "Well, you can stay at my place if you want to. If you don't mind sharing a futon. I wake up early."

"Really? Are you sure? I feel so stupid." There was something rehearsed about the question, as if this was what she had been expecting all along.

———

"Did you sleep with her?" Sonya wanted to know when he gave her his weekly wrap-up, his customary five-minute "state of the self" address.

"Yeah, well, she slept on my futon because she couldn't get into her place until morning."

She gave him her death-ray stare with her coal black eyes, her stop-bullshitting look. She had an appetite for the gritty details. "Did you have sex, I mean?"

He paused. "I'm afraid so."

"Why afraid? That's what you wanted, wasn't it? You didn't enjoy it?"

"Oh, well . . . Yes, but I thought I was dropping her off, and she said she forgot her keys, and . . . it wasn't expected, or planned."

Sonya shrugged. "When is it? Sex happens when it wants. Either through desire or weakness."

"Or both." He chuckled. She gave him "the look" again, inhaled deeply on her cigarette, and stubbed it out, halfway done, adding it to the collection of its predecessors in the ashtray—a little birch grove of half-smoked Kents. How could he tell her he had been perfectly willing—eager—to fall asleep, was halfway there, but Alice kept fidgeting in the bed, and she was wearing his pajamas, and then her leg fell across his, and her hand landed on his upper thigh, and then her lips were upon him, doing their soft, sweet magic, and then she was suddenly naked, warm pale flesh, her breasts bare in the moonlight (meant for someone else), her eyes closed like shells, her full strong midwestern ass rising and falling in his hands?

"I haven't been with anyone in months," he said to Sonya, by way of explanation. He left out the midspring tryst with Hannah Gold, the rabbi's lusty daughter.

She shrugged. "You're a grown man—physically. You can do what you want. Do you miss her—what's her name—the Italian?"

Her question had suddenly conjured Alexis, sum-moned and stirred up the coconut-scented perfume she wore, a tiny vial of which he had found in his room and now kept on his desk and partook of now and then to re-activate his overactive capacity for nostalgia. Her skin was kind of a tawny, yellow brown which turned an even darker brown at the first hint of spring; he missed the way she smiled and sort of growled before she was going to pounce, and the last time they made love it was the middle part of a soft spring afternoon, a few weeks after she had left him for the stockbroker. Now that it was illicit, their lovemaking had regained its tenderness, and after-ward, he leaned out the window and watched her bicycle away, blue dress wavering in the breeze, as in a movie by Fellini.

"Alexis? Oh, sort of—not the fighting part. Maybe the . . . other parts. I still talk to her. Every week or two. She's with some English stockbroker who drinks too much and locks her out. Then she calls me crying. My old girl-friends really love me—*after* we break up. And then, they think I'm some kind of love expert."

"She wants you back?"

"No, just free advice, and sympathy. He makes love bet-ter anyway, I'm told."

"For now, maybe yes. Then someone else will do it bet-ter."

Sonya was building up to something, he could tell, a pronouncement of some sort. "Why do you stay in touch with them," she asked, "these old girlfriends?"

"I still love them."

"For sex?"

"No—I don't sleep with them. Just to talk to. I miss them. How can you just let them go, forever?"

She flashed the blue tattoo on the pale, fishlike under-belly of her arm. She shrugged. "Life is too short—you can't hold on. They will hold you back. Remember—time and energy," she repeated, her favorite mantra, "that's all we have. What if, after the war, I had just thought only of Auschwitz—my family, all dead! I couldn't survive, couldn't function! Or after my first husband died, then my second! We all have to live in the present." Like many things Sonya said, it was hard to argue with: she had the credentials of hardship.

He had heard the whole story, too, her family rounded up in the small Polish village, the ghetto, then the trains, separation from her parents—executed, with all siblings but one—four years in the camps as a teenager and young woman, the forced march away from the Allies, and then, with others, miraculous escape to the forest, bullets in the trees, a long walk to Austria, somehow to Israel, then America, where she spoke not a word of English. She enrolled in graduate school anyway, finished in three years, started a practice, met her husband on a street corner, bought the house in which they now sat.

"But enough about me—how about you? How do you think you're progressing these days?"

"Oh, well—not tearing up the pea patch, but I think I have a little more focus than I did before." He was treading lightly in the self-congratulation department. "At least I'm in school, and have some idea where I'm heading." Sonya looked skeptical.

She was staring again, had fixed him in her gaze, vaguely smiling. "I don't know about your pea patch, but, well, now . . . at least you're on a path." Unlike his parents, Sonya was capable of both withering criticism and sudden bursts of sunlit optimism.

"I think it will be wonderful! And when you get your Ph.D.—and a nice job, you will be soooooo happy!" She gazed at him for a moment longer, then stood up and opened the door and called down the stairs: "Annie, please, more poison! Trevor, good-bye. Alphonse, are you there? Come up—hurry. I'm still here! Come. Quick!"

Then it was November. Overnight, the oak trees that framed his view of the river lost their leaves; the nights turned brittle and cold and left a skin of hoary frost on the lawn that would melt away at the first blur of sunlight. One Saturday morning he crawled under the old car with a hammer, a pair of pliers and some wire and—in a trick shown to him by his VW mechanic back in Cheshire—banged and pulled and moved two levers of the heat boxes, tied them back with wire, and there—the heat was turned on for the season. So much satisfaction for a little task! On a long drive, the car would get so warm he'd have to open the windows to cool down.

New York does well at the holidays, and even before Thanksgiving there was a distant jangle of Christmas in the air. His courses marched on, comforting and dull, most of the work consisted of typing weekly "response papers" to the readings and the lectures that would come back with a few scrawled queries or comments. He and Sydney and hippie Joey prepared a theatrical adaptation of a Hemingway story for the class in the apartment of Sydney's parents, who, he was astonished to discover, were full-fledged Germans, their accents so thick they could hardly be understood, which offered an explanation for Sydney's overwrought Americanness, his thick accent culled from late-night movies. The apartment was full of glass and silver and precious European artifacts. They practiced their skit, and got drunk on fancy cognac.

After his initial flurry of possibility with Daya, she had been hard to find, or catch up to after class, and foolishly, he had never taken down her number. One day before her class he stopped by her dorm, asked the uninterested young man at the desk if he knew her, but he could now not remember her last name. "We have a lot of Africans here. I need more information," said the dimwit, and went back to reading his tired copy of *The Chronicles of Narnia*. But then as he left the building, Daya was rushing in.

"I was just looking for you. I haven't been able to find you after class."

"Oh, hi. Yeah, I've been still working," she explained. "I was wondering what happened to you, too." She invited him in, and they ascended together in a tiny elevator to her suite, inhabited by a giggling Indian in a sari who was busy cooking and seemed never to have seen a man in their apartment before. Daya's room was small, but tidy, and he sat on the bed and watched her gather her things for class. Always pleasant, this first incursion into a woman's room, the first barrier breached. "You can come back for dinner, sometime, if you want to," she said as they hustled out. "Soon, my night job will be over."

They arrived almost late to class, then sat near to but not next to each other, no doubt causing a raised eyebrow from Sydney across the room. Afterward, he drifted over to him. "Coming, old boy? We're going for a cocktail: after that scintillating performance by our lady professor, a giant in her field," he said, rolling his eyes, "I think I will need several."

"No thanks," he begged off, "maybe Friday. I think I need to get some sleep."

"Sleep, eh? Is that *all* you need?" There was the eyebrow, slightly raised.

They drifted off, and Daya was still beside him. "Don't you have to go to your night job?" he asked her.

"Not tonight. I told them I had to study."

"In that case, do you want to get a drink somewhere—not with the crew, maybe, but somewhere else?"

They walked down Amsterdam a couple more blocks to a small corner bistro next to St. John the Divine. Daya was a bit dressed up, it seemed to him, and her lips shone with a kind of ruby gloss that reminded him of someone, but whom? By candlelight, her skin had taken on a deep rich warmth of brown, and she had combed her hair up into an even higher Afro. When they stepped outside into the darkness, something cold kissed his face, and with a thrill of childhood he looked up into the streetlight where a few sparks were falling through the light. "Uh-oh," he said. "Here comes something." She too was thrilled—never had seen snow before, except at her uncle's farm, once, high in the mountains in the south. They walked over to Morningside Heights, overlooking the lights of Harlem, glittering beneath them as the octagonal paving stones underfoot accepted a dusting of white. He had already looped his arm through hers, and she somehow guided him to an enormous tree, and turned to face him. A cap of snow had gathered on her hair, and he brushed it off, and he watched a flake land on the warm skin of her upper breast, melt there, and slide away. A new look had come onto her face. "What?" he asked, took her by the waist. She looked nervous, and shy, her same white boots padding a packed place in the snow. Her lip quavered, as if she was fighting back tears. "I wish you could kiss me," she suggested. "I want to, now."

And then there was the cold; the background hiss of falling snow; the warmth and wetness of her lips; the texture of her hair he was clutching as they kissed, his fingers kneading and clutching, like something he had known all his life but forgotten; there was the weight and warmth and softness of her body as it was pressed between him and the rough, cold bark of the tree. The darkness was all around them, and underfoot was the warm white glow of snow. These were the things he would remember. It was a long time before they stopped and paused, toes succumbing to the snow they were standing on, and she said, her feet nervously padding the ground, as they had the first time he had seen her in class, "I wish you would come over." And without an answer they had walked through the falling snow in the general direction of her room.

It was not until the following day, back in his own town, in the cocoon of his own two rooms, on his futon on the floor, looking up at the branches of the pines where an inch or two of snow still lay, knocked off in cascading clumps by boisterous blue jays, that he remembered he had agreed to go to the movie with Alice that very night. How to explain it? After months of loneliness, involuntary chastity, countless solitary nights in a city bursting with young and lonely women, he found himself in a small romantic conundrum. He was pleasantly weary and happy with the night spent with Daya, wanted no further complications, but it was too late to cancel; the movie, he feared, would lead to the Moonlight Mile, and the Moonlight Mile would provide them with pitchers of beer, and she would laugh, and look pretty, and her breasts would swell upward toward him, and her apartment would still be just across the street, with the swirling cats, and her nice firm bed, with its clean white sheet, and naked Alice between them. But it was too late to cancel.

And so it had gone according to script. The movie was bad, but provided many laughs afterward, in the bar, fueled by the beer she kept ordering, against his protestations. By the time he had gotten to her door, he had beaten his qualms into submission by force-fed recollection of his lonely Brooklyn existence—a rolling catalog of all the beautiful women he had desired, over the years, but would never have, had never even touched, including all those high school girls on the subway and the fabulous bank teller, Darlene Dargen, whom he would hover over every time he extracted his twenty-five dollars. And wasn't it his own mother who had often said, "Make hay while the sun shines"? Besides, how many times would he be able to say he had shared the beds of different women on consecutive nights? He also knew both relationships were in the embryonic stage, at the mercy of the whims and vicissitudes of fortune, did not know whither either was tending. By the following Tuesday, for all he knew, he might be back on his own again, marching across the lonely bachelor's desert. Like camels, you could never be certain where the next sip of water might be coming from.

By one in the morning, the drama had unfolded satisfactorily, and come to a desired conclusion, with Alice asleep—the dull glow of the clock beside the bed said 1:03 a.m. And although now, after two nights away, he was longing for his own futon, and aloneness, it seemed poor etiquette to leave at one in the morning, so he clung to the edge of the bed and forced himself to sleep until a weak gray light was coming through the window, and the sight of her two vaguely malevolent cats started swirling, stirring the air. He dozed fitfully until 5:31, kissed her on the cheek, and murmured good-bye, and he was into his clothes in a hurry, down the carpeted stairs, and out into the quiet street of the town. He went to the local deli, run by Greeks or Armenians, bought a garlic bagel and a coffee for one dollar, and began to consume them as he walked the half mile home. Ah, the sweet, immeasurable pleasures of New York!

"I'm shocked!" Sonya said, stood up, then, as quickly, sat down. He thought it might have been a mistake to tell her— so why had he?

"I didn't sleep with both of them—make love, I mean. Only Alice, from town." It was true. Although he had shared a single bed with Daya the night before, they had shed some of their clothes but not all and worked on their kissing and, as if to explain her reluctance to go further, she had said, "It feels like we just met."

"We did," he said, "so let's sleep," a suggestion she immediately took him up on. He woke with a crick in his neck, to the smell of scrambled eggs and toast she had made, shared with the Indian woman who seemed excited by the presence of a man in their suite, especially at eight in the morning. They had kissed good-bye, chastely but on the lips, and he had promised he would call her later.

Sonya shrugged. "You stayed with two women on the same weekend?"

"Well, yes, but we're just friends, at this point."

"Friends? That's what you call people you have sex with?" Sonya wanted to know. "I think this is more than a friend. I have heard this expression, 'Friends with benefits.' I don't like it. 'Benefits'—maybe that's good for the animals," she growled, "but not for human beings!"

It was time to steer the conversation into safer waters, but it was too late.

"And what about the other—the African? Do you like her?"

"Yes, I do actually—she's interesting."

"Because she's *different*?"

Trevor was not very political, but knew what she was getting at. Sonya raised her hand: "I'm just asking."

"I don't believe so."

"Maybe you're competing with your sister," Sonya suggested. "She's with a Brazilian, and now you're doing her one better—an African." She seemed to like the sound of the word.

He had been reluctant to tell her about Daya, for when he had told her, weeks before, that his older sister was engaged to a Brazilian, she had asked, "A Black?"

"Well, brown," Trevor had rejoined, and Sonya had answered, oddly, "Why would she want to do a thing like that?"

"Maybe she loves him." He said it softly, and perhaps flushed, and Sonya could see she was on uncertain terrain. She held up a hand again: "Don't get me wrong, Trevor. There's nothing wrong with it. But life is hard enough—but when you are with someone from another culture, of another color—even more problems. Sometimes, love is not enough. But, well, if it works out, I'll dance at their wedding!!"

Sonya herself had already outlived two husbands—a successful doctor and a businessman who, though both Jewish, could nonetheless not survive their vibrant wife. With one of them, she had produced a son, a limp and feckless lawyer who called her constantly in the middle of his sessions, for guidance and approval.

"I'm not a bigot," she clarified—"remember, my whole family—gone! Thank you, very much, Mr. Hitler! But life is not easy—why create more . . . difficulties. It's hard enough being with someone even when they are . . . from the same place, culture, religion. . . ." She was being careful, again. And then she abruptly stopped, smiled at him, her ruby smile, powdered cheeks, black hair that rose in its magic way above her head, and gazed at him.

"Anyway, you're getting a little sex. Good for you. Don't make a baby. What else? Tell me something . . . more, interesting. How's school?"

He had been getting the feeling lately that there was less and less to tell her, less and less that was new, and that, like a horse on a tether, he was beating the same path around and around the same dusty pasture; perhaps *their* romance, too, was coming to a close. Sonya was not much interested in the past, in his parents, why he felt the way he did about himself, what events, traumatic and mundane, from his childhood, had caused him to be the way he was. "If we had a thousand years," she had said once, "yes, we could go over all that, like archaeologists, but we don't. That's the problem with Freud—there's no time." She shrugged: "Plus, it's all over—we can't change the past," she said, and then added— "but . . . we can influence the future." She raised a single finger of triumph and stood up: it was time to go.

Then it was Thanksgiving: he went home, but did not stay for the weekend as usual, taking long walks with the dog and looking up old friends; instead he returned on Friday evening, on the pretense of schoolwork. In truth, he wanted to return to make sure the spark of possibility with Daya was not left unattended for too long. She had seemed surprised when, before he left, he had suggested she come visit his family for a day or two before Christmas. There was going to be a little party for his older sister and João, her fiancé, with a couple of December birthdays tacked on. She had no family here, was his thinking, would be spending Christmas alone or with friends, might like to get outside the city and see what America was like up in the country. "But it's your *family*," she had said. "Do they know about me?"

"That we're friends, and you're from Zimbabwe, and you're new to the country, and . . ."

"That I'm Black?"

"Well, Zimbabwe . . . I assume they understand. You know, they're those nice liberal White folks you read about—the ones with only subtle racial issues."

"Well, we have lots of Europeans too, White Africans, the settlers. Now they're all running up from South Africa, buying up land, clinging to their way of life."

"Besides," he added, "most White Americans love Africans—it's their own countrymen they're scared of."

"Including you?"

"Hmmm . . ." He was working hard to be honest here. "To some extent, probably. You don't have to spend the night if you don't want. I can put you on a train in the afternoon. But you'll have your own room."

"Oh, well. As long as they know about me, that's all. In my country, you don't invite someone home until you've known them a long time. And, you know, you're serious." He decided not to take her up on that one.

In turn, she had invited him to a party at the college the following weekend—a fund- and consciousness-raiser for divestment from South Africa. He had arrived alone, and for some time stood alone at the bar nursing a Tusker beer, with a picture of an elephant on it. Then he found her, finally, and she introduced him to some of her friends, pleasantly but formally, but then she was drawn away into various ardent conversations, and so he hovered by the bar, drinking, attempting to talk to anyone standing nearby, but nothing took root. Daya would reappear now and then, but after a few words she got pulled away. And then music started, and he watched her dance, subtly and sensually, with other men. She invited him to join her, and he did, but was put off by the glimpse of himself in a mirror—a pale, awkward stick man in a sea of brown faces, people who knew how to dance—and after one song he thanked her and returned to the safety of the bar. It took him a while to admit that he was getting either angry or hurt, he wasn't certain which. When it was time to leave, he considered going without telling her, but then finally waved and told her he had to go. It was a long drive, he said, and she followed him to the door, and then out into cold late-November air.

"I'll talk to you tomorrow," he said outside the hall. "Go back and have fun."

"Are you running away from me?"

"No, but it seems like you have lots of friends in there, or weren't sure if you wanted to be seen with me."

"Why do you say that?" she asked, still walking beside him. It occurred to him that she was, if not drunk, then tipsy; her words had taken on rounded edges and were blurring into each other.

"Because you left me alone all night at the bar. I don't know anyone there."

"They're my friends," she said, "They're very political—they're all worked up about this divestment thing . . . apartheid . . . trying to organize, talking about boycotting classes." She paused, and they stopped in the quiet, cold shadow of a chapel, as if for protection from something. "They were making me nervous. They kept asking me about you, if we were together, saying things. . . ."

"Like what?"

"Just subtle things, you know, asking about your 'politics,' where you are from, if your parents knew about me, stuff like that. . . ."

"Tell them I don't have any politics, or parents. I'm a hick from the country, raised by wolves."

She tried to smile. Then she was quiet, biting her lip, looking away with eyes softened by tears.

"What's the matter?"

"Just me!" she said suddenly, not loudly but clearly, stamping her foot in protest against some unseen thing. Her feet were padding the stones, again, stepping in place. "Just me!" she repeated. "I want you to like me because of me, just me—not because I'm African, or Black, or exotic, or something, just like me because you like me—Daya, a poor girl from the village who likes to read books. Now I'm lost in this big place . . . !" she protested, and he watched her face, lovely and sad, fighting against her own sorrow, until his own eyes had filled with tears. She was standing apart from him, at a safe distance, in protest, staring off onto the echoing, empty campus—footsteps and voices on the stones.

"Just you?" he asked, and pulled her into his arms.

"Yes, just me!" she repeated, not responding, resisting, rooted to the earth.

He inched closer. "Just you?"

"Yes." she said, losing steam. "Now you're teasing." She leaned against him and started to weep. "All those people, they keep asking me—are you together, is he your boy-friend? Why did you bring him? Gosh!! I'm tired of this place—too many questions, too complicated."

And when it had stopped, she wiped her eyes and looked at him. "Are you my boyfriend? I think I need to know what to tell them."

"If you want me to be."

"What do you want?"

"To be with . . . a smart girl . . . from the village. . . ."

"An African village?"

"If that's where she's from, yes."

She was looking back at him with her soft doe eyes, not speaking.

"Just you?" he asked, touched by the sadness of the ques-tion.

"Yes, only me," she repeated, and tried to smile. "I'm tired. Maybe I drank too much wine." She was trying to be brave.

". . . who likes books?"

"Yes," she said, looking down at the ground. "Good books."

"From the village?"

"Yes, a nice village . . ." She bit her lower lip, and her eyes refilled with tears.

"What?" he asked. "What's the matter?"

"I miss home," she said, wearily, and then added, as if she had just remembered, "I miss my mother!" It was less a comment than a lamentation, the wellspring of sorrow she had just tapped into, and now came flowing forth. "I miss my mother!!" she repeated, with more urgency now, as a kind of wail, and as he pulled her toward him she gave up her resistance, finally, collapsed against him, and then broke down altogether, pulling him back toward her, sobbing in his arms like a child.

December had come upon them suddenly, a final flurry of papers and presentations and things to be done. His car had fulfilled its potential for disaster on his way back from Sonya's one frigid snowless Monday: the clutch pedal fell to the floor like a dead fish, and he pulled over on the Brooklyn-Queens Expressway, in plain sight of both the Tastee sign and the skeletal globe from the World's Fair. The car was still running; the clutch pedal lay on the floor. On a whim of panic and inspiration, he jumped back in, turned off the engine, pressed the shift into first, and turned the key, and the car lurched forward, spluttered, and caught, and he drove down the breakdown lane: then with a kind of thrill he discovered, clutch or no clutch, he could still drive, ease the shift into second, then third, which was fast enough to get him home—with one scary moment at the tolls when he had to turn off the car and start the process all over again.

The next day he got a new clutch cable, but a day later the starter motor wouldn't work, so he walked to town for coffee, came back an hour later, and the car started without a problem. The man at the gas station shrugged. "There are worse problems," he said. "If you need a new one, let us know—but it could give you the same problem. They're all recycled anyway."

Sonya was unimpressed. "Maybe you need a better car." She shrugged. He did not tell her that he had invited Daya to come home with him to visit his family before Christmas, as he knew it would be read with her old-world eyes—an introduction to the family, laden with overtones and meaning. Rather, he saw his family as a kind of trump card, another feather in his cap—kind and friendly parents, divorced but happily reconfigured, jolly siblings who liked to drink and laugh; the handsome, understated house.

On the morning of their departure he woke to the sight of large white flakes of snow falling down toward him, settling on the branches of the pine tree outside his window. The forecast, as seen on his newly bought black-and-white TV, was for continued snow, clearing in the afternoon. He would have to drive thirty minutes south first to pick her up, and then back onto the highway winding north again, into Connecticut. He could call and ask her to take the 1 train to the Bronx, but that would be unchivalric, and he didn't know her well enough to start making demands. Better just to go, risk it, as Sonya would have him do—live, be bold—if the car broke, fix it or, better yet, get a new one! Go, go, go!

He got dressed quickly, went outside, wiped the snow off the car's roof and windshield, climbed in, and—tick, tick, tick—the starter motor kicked in with a lusty growl, sent a plume of blue smoke out the back. He turned on his radio to its staticky, AM best, reversed with a satisfying crunch and compression into the snow, then forward around the front of the house.

The streets of the town—the "village"—were covered still, and he kept the engine revving at the two red lights, for fear of stalling, and passed up his usual deli for coffee in favor of a gas station on the outskirts of town: if the car died, they could get him going again, but it didn't. He pulled out onto River Road, heading south. It, too, was yet unplowed, and the snow was coming down harder now, and the car in front of him was only two red sparks dimly seen through the white. He considered turning around, finding a phone booth to call, but south of Yonkers the sky brightened briefly, then closed in again. There were two grooves of packed snow for the wheels, but if he drifted and got into the soft stuff, the car would start to swerve and shimmy. He heard on the radio something about four to six inches, finishing around noon—not a blizzard, exactly, but they strongly advised everyone to stay off the roads. Blue lights ahead, on the right!! He slowed but kept his momentum, peered over the edge, where a moving van had skidded off and over an embankment, plowed up against a bale of hay.

The snow was heavier, and the flakes would rush at the windshield and then, in that magical moment of childhood, at the last possible instant swoop up and over the car. He wound his way through the familiar, swoopy turns of the Bronx, Riverdale, and over the Harlem River, his car wavering on the metal grid, the coal black river below. The Henry Hudson was not much better, only one lane advisable for traffic, though in typical New York fashion, cars kept pressing past him on the left, veering and swerving and leaving him in an impenetrable snowy cloud. "Idiot New Yorkers," he muttered to himself, reverting to regional prejudice. It would be foolish to go now—Daya would understand. He would find somewhere to park, plow into a snowbank, and spend the day with her, in bed, perhaps, hunkered down against the storm.

When he got to her dorm he double-parked, left the engine running, and dashed into the dorm to explain. Idiot boy was still there, on to a new book, and handed him the phone without comment. "I'm here," he said into the receiver, "but it's snowing, and I don't think we—"

"I'll be right down." He waited by the car, and she climbed in, holding a bag that smelled of food and coffee.

"I don't think we should go," he said. "It's still snowing hard, and I don't know how it's going to be up there, and besides, I'm still worried about my starter motor—if we have to stop to get gas, I have to turn off the engine, and if it won't start, we won't be able to jump-start it, and . . ."

She looked puzzled. "But it's working now, right? It's going. You drove it here? Plus, your family is expecting us, aren't they?" She did not grasp the perils involved—the problem of the snow, the mechanics of jump-starting, and general unreliability, and his own well-proven capacity for apprehension. "Ah, let's go," she said happily. "I think it will be fine. An adventure. I brought you some coffee. Wait until I get settled, and . . ."

There, it was decided. He didn't know her well enough to throw a little fit of resistance, and so, relieved from being himself, he pushed the car into first and took off up Amsterdam, left, right, north along the Henry Hudson, back over the bridge and then through the two sweeping turns that passed through Yonkers, up and over a hill, and then past the exit that would lead them back to his house. "Last chance . . . we can still chicken out."

"Oh, no—you're fine." She patted him on the knee. From her bag she brought forth a thermos of coffee and a cup, which she half filled and handed to him. Traffic was moving at forty or so, and he had settled in comfortably behind a Jeep, tugging them along in its snowy wake.

But as he passed the exit to Irvington he thought of Alice, still sleeping in her bed, her guard cats keeping watch. The end of their tryst had come with a whimper not a bang, over the telephone: the week after the party with Daya they had spoken, he had told her he had been to an "African party" on the weekend with a friend, and she had said, perhaps gleaning a romantic subtext, "What kind of music did they play, jungle beat?" She laughed her tingly laugh, and he let her, but the ugliness of the comment resonated over the line, and he wondered if this is what passed for humor at Williams College: in any case, it served as the final and useful ingredient to solidify his resolve, and the next time they went to the movies he skipped the beer at the Moonlight Mile, pleading weariness and papers to write, and dropped her off in front of her house. Did she look wistful, or was that just his ego and imagination? When he leaned over to kiss her good night, she offered only her cheek—touché!! He would let her have the last word, and the illusion that she had ended it. Nonetheless, she had now joined the modest pantheon, known to him alone, of ex- and almost girlfriends.

To change the subject in his head he started talking, gave Daya the rundown of the family members she could expect to meet—siblings, mother, stepfather, father probably, though without his wife, who, despite ten years of getting used to it, was still allergic to family gatherings, probably due to lingering guilt syndrome for breaking up the marriage. And then João, the handsome Brazilian who, it was suspected, had something important to say regarding his intentions toward his oldest sister.

"And your parents won't have any problems with it?" Daya asked. "Because he's from Brazil, and you said he's darker—brown?"

"No, they like him—plus, she was with a lot of older creeps in the past, bearded hippie types who spent all her money. He's younger and happy and treats her well, so they're happy."

"And they know I'm coming, right?"

"Yes, dear—separate bedrooms, don't worry."

"I'm not worried—just don't want to give anyone a shock."

As they growled north he could feel the city falling away behind him, its great stony weight receding, and with it his own apprehensions seemed to dissipate, as if he himself was growing lighter, as if this journey foreshadowed his own inevitable escape from the city. "It's beautiful, isn't it?" Daya said. She seemed happy too, to be moving, somewhere, anywhere, away. Even his crappy radio, away from the electronic congestion of the city, had perked up and found some stations in southern Connecticut. The gas gauge was below half.

"We still have to get gas," he reminded himself, not wanting to let down his guard. "I don't want to turn the engine off, but they say the car can blow up, and . . ."

"At home, we always leave it running," Daya said. "I think it will be fine."

When they got to his favorite truck stop below Waterbury, she went inside to pee and pay the ten dollars he had given her for gas: he stayed put and pumped with the engine running, braced for explosion, but there was none.

"See," Daya said, a cap of white snow on her hair, emerging with a bag of good stuff to see them through the final hour—another coffee, a sticky bun, a bag of peanuts— the kinds of small pleasures he was good at denying himself. "You have to be nice to yourself," Sonya had told him more than once. "If you aren't, how can you take care of someone else?" He had not even told her about Sonya yet—his need for guidance.

She had also bought a couple bottles of soda and juice to take to his family, another nicety he would have thought of and ignored.

"You can't go empty-handed," Daya said. "At home we called them 'guests with no hands' because they arrive with them in their pockets. Ah"—she laughed—"it's considered quite disgraceful."

For a time, when they were purring along in fourth, she had taken his hand in hers, less holding than laying one upon the other for company. The gesture, it occurred to him, would have annoyed him with previous girlfriends, set off internal bells of alarm as too romantic, but now it had the opposite effect, seemed to settle him, calm him down, connected him to something beyond his own skittish self. Although it had not stopped snowing since they left, the driving had not gotten any worse or better—because, he theorized, they were traveling along with the storm, riding a wave, the brave blue car surfing north on a great soft crush of snow.

When they reached the Cheshire exit, only half an hour slower than usual, his heart quickened with his boyhood thrill of return—back from summer camp; from college; back from aimless peregrinations in Europe, from tussles with real life in the Big Apple. "It's beautiful," Daya said, "like those postcards you see." And so it was—the white church, the town "green," the tidy main street, falling snow. Left, right, left: the familiar streets fell away before him like dominoes, and then he was turning onto the old country lane, between the familiar gap in the stone wall, and into the driveway where a familiar cluster of cars had already assembled, pulled up willy-nilly in the unplowed snow, each parked in the particular style of his siblings. Although the sky had lightened, their arrival coincided with a final burst of snowfall, thick and white and swirling.

"Well, we made it!" Daya said triumphantly, patting the dashboard. "Thanks to your car, and your good driving, of course. You must be tired. You can rest now."

"And thanks to you, too," he said, relieved. "Remember—I wasn't even going to come." She had pressed them onward, given him courage when he had begun to falter.

From the back door of the house had emerged his older sister, looking more and more like their mother; then João with his beautiful teeth, skin golden against the snow, handsomer than he remembered. "Come," she said, excited, and climbed out of the car, and then, as if in a movie he was watching, she quickly covered the distance between them, arms spread for balance, introduced herself to each with a handshake, then a sudden hug, as though they had all met before somewhere. They looked at him in his car, someone said something, and they laughed, silver plumes of breath swirling in unison, snow gathering on their clothes and hair. Daya looked and waved and indicated they were going inside, and for him to come, as if *he* was the visitor. He waved back—he was coming—and they disappeared into the house, to the drinks and crackers and oysters and laughter, olives and celery sticks, the huddled warmth of family.

He turned off the car and it spluttered to silence, just a few odd ticks of it cooling. He could hear the individual snowflakes landing on the windshield and roof, gathering, one on top of the other, not melting. His body tingled, still thrumming with motion, momentum, a million tiny explosions that had powered them there. He took his bag from the back and started to get out, then stopped. He slipped the key back into the ignition and turned, but nothing happened—not even the tick tick tick of the starter motor, trying. There was only the sound of snowflakes on the windshield, adding to the whiteness. He turned the key again, and again, but still there was no other sound—only the snowflakes and the silence, silence all around.

The Last of the Caribs

It wasn't much of a car, he could tell, an old, tired Nissan rented from the owner of the guesthouse where he was staying—107,000 kilometers, the odometer read, or was it miles? It was hot in the car, and the air conditioner didn't work, but the engine started with a throaty gurgle, and he sat for a moment in idle, working through the gears with his left hand, adjusting to the right-hand drive. He was about to pull out when he felt, suddenly, that he had forgotten something, but what? His camera lay on the seat beside him, and with it a map of the island. But the world was too bright and glaring: sunglasses! He slapped his pockets, then leaped out of the car and ran up the rickety stairs to his tiny, dreary room and found them, on his bed—a fancy leather case with the words "Giovanni and Ferrera" scripted into the jet-black leather. The case opened and shut with a satisfying snap, the beautifully made sunglasses held safely inside, like a naked woman in a coffin. He slipped them into his pocket, ran down to the car, opened all the windows, and lurched out into the busy, sunstruck streets of the scruffy Caribbean town with the pretty French name: Roseau.

He drove carefully, crept slowly around the block, turned left again, and then headed down the main street, out of town. He had just passed over the river and was getting used to driving on the left when he saw a couple he had met on the plane—a skinny Rasta guy and his White American girlfriend—and in an effort to wave he took his eye off the road and got too close to the edge, and his rear wheel slammed down into a culvert with a loud, discomforting sound of metal on concrete. Out on the street, people looked, but he kept moving. "Take it easy, red man!" someone shouted from a passing car, glaring. Martin waved in apology. The couple from the plane glanced over in the direction of the car, and disappeared around the corner.

"Red man," was it? He had traveled enough in the Caribbean to know that this was neither an insult nor a term of endearment, exactly, but something in between—a statement of fact. He glanced at his face in the rearview mirror: it *was* red, actually, or at least pink from walking around the day before. He had forgotten any form of sunblock, as was his custom, risking skin cancer for the satisfaction of a deep, reddish tan—angry thumbprint of the sun.

As the road wound out of the town, the traffic eased. The smooth, glittering sea spread out to his left in the ineffable blue-green hues of the Caribbean, and to his right the great green mass of the island rose steeply upward in a thicket of trees and weeds and undergrowth, a junglelike profusion. As a teacher of history and social studies back in America, he didn't find it hard to imagine its grisly past—the English and French and Spanish as they thrashed their way around the island in their shiny metal suits and helmets, bearing swords and pikes and guns in their mad pursuit of each other, or their escaped African slaves, or the Caribs themselves, who, purged from other islands, had been granted a kind of halfhearted refuge here, reprieve from the genocidal attentions of the White man. They had settled on the far side of the island on land which had eventually been given to them as the "Carib Territory," and it was there that he was now uneasily headed, in his rented car, winding up the narrow road through rows and rows of trees bearing a strange blue fruit—bananas wrapped in plastic bags to protect them, he guessed, from marauding insects. There, too, were trees with shiny leaves laden with breadfruit and pendulous mangoes, ripening on the branches with a strange, erotic fullness. It was still hot in the car, passing in and out of sunlight and shade, and driving on the left was not easy. In his rearview mirror minibuses would suddenly appear, honking and flashing their lights, and he would pull over and wave them past.

The road passed over an aqua-colored river and forked at a large mango tree, and he took a right and headed steeply uphill, squinting into sudden light. Sunglasses. He reached quickly down to his pocket, snapped open the fancy leather case, and lifted them out. They were wonderfully light and fine, the frames made of a kind of airplane alloy, with miraculously precise hinges, glass of a pale green which rendered the world cooler, clear, precise. Even *he* looked better in them, glimpsed in the rearview mirror, vaguely rakish, though slightly more like a tourist than he would have liked. They were a type he would not have worn back in America—more stylish, perhaps, than his modest looks warranted—but he would get used to them, wear them on special occasions, keep them in his top drawer at home and claim to his wife that, sunstruck and feeling extravagant, he had bought them for himself.

"Don't lose them," he had been advised by the woman who had given them to him. "They were expensive."

How expensive could they be? One hundred dollars? Two? He tended not to buy expensive things for himself, but loved having these, loved the way they sat on his nose, loved their titanium frames and perfect silent hinges and the way the world looked through them, the way he felt in them, like someone slightly other than himself—someone more daring, more handsome, someone who had just had an adulterous romance at the summer conference he had been attending on another island, St. Lucia, learning things he could then impart to his uninterested students back in America. The sunglasses had come as a gift, in parting, wrapped in a beautiful box, a memento of all their time together. They made him uneasy, too, as he tended to lose things he cared about—held on so tightly to them that they fled of their own accord: objects, people, time itself. Already he missed her with a dull, ache that would not go away. Sunglasses, though, he could hold on to forever, smuggle them back to America and take them out for skiing, maybe, a trip to the beach, a long drive with his wife and daughter.

No, not the beach: oddly, one of his earliest and unhappiest memories involved a pair of sunglasses—small plastic ones with a cowboy motif, with little pistols perched jauntily on the frames. He must have been only three or four, and had taken them to the beach one hot summer day, and on the way to the parking lot they had somehow become lost in the sand, and he remembered his desperate and futile search—his sunburned back, his frazzled and exhausted mother urging him to hurry, to give it up, and finally the rage and injustice of it all as he trudged to the car, bawling and defeated, the bitter car ride home. How he had loved those tiny cowboy sunglasses! Where had they gone? Swallowed by sand.

By the end of the eighteenth century, he had read during the conference, "the European arrivals in the Lesser Antilles found territories sparsely inhabited, for the most part, by the warlike Caribs, who frequently opposed their intrusion.

Many an uprising took place, but, by the end of the century, a fairly general pattern had been established; the Caribs were decimated or expelled, moving to Dominica and St. Vincent. An area of 3,700 acres of land on the north of the east coast of the island has been given to the descendants of the original inhabitants of the Caribbean islands—the Carib Indians. Today the Caribs engage in agriculture, fishing, and their native crafts of dugout canoe and basket making." Why was he so intent on visiting there in the first place—why had he taken a three-day detour on his way home—he who had seldom taken much interest in the indigenous peoples of North America, where he lived? The conference where he had just spent a single summer month, reading and discussing the history of the Americas, had now and then mentioned the Caribs and Arawaks and Tainos in passing, but these people, it was agreed, once Europeans had arrived, didn't fare very well, died off by the thousands: disease, war, suicide, a reluctance to be enslaved and do the work of the red-faced men with the guns and metal suits and the snarling, salivating mastiffs who would chase them down in the forests and rip them to shreds when they escaped. A couple of summers before, on yet another island, he had stood with his wife and then-two-year-old daughter on the edge of a cliff, "Carib's Leap"—a lonely and windswept place at the end of a beautiful cemetery where the last of the Caribs had leaped to the rocks and the sea below, preferring death to a life of misery and subjugation and enslavement. Others fled in their dugout canoes, paddled north to Dominica, where, they had been told, they would be left alone, and there, for three hundred years, they had remained.

He had hoped to give someone a ride in exchange for directions and company, but so far there had been no one on the road—a few children watching him pass, women at work carrying bundles of bananas on their heads, two men with

machetes. According to the map he would reach a confluence of four roads, a rotary, of sorts, at the top of the island,
near the boiling lake, where he would have a choice to
make: take a left, toward the airport, and then take the road
south, through Carib Territory, or go straight and approach
from the north. It was hard to tell which would be better.
He was mindful of the time, wanted to get the car back by
five, didn't want to be driving along these narrow, winding
roads after dark, and so drove with a gathering sense of urgency. But then the car growled up a final ascent, flattened
off, and there he was, at a crossroads, a confusing jumble of
signs pointing in various directions—toward the boiling
lake, or to the island's great waterfall, or back to Roseau
and his scruffy little guesthouse there, with its creaking single bed. A woman sat at a kind of booth, selling flowers, and
another group at a bus stop, studying his car. He pulled
slowly up to them, slid off his sunglasses, and asked a young,
dark-skinned man which was the best way to Carib Territory.

"This way." The man pointed, and asked quickly, "You
going there?"

"I hope so," Martin said. "Do you want a ride?"

"Yeah, man," he said, and then turned to look back hopefully at the three others—two women and one man—who
were waiting with him.

"Can they fit?" Martin asked, and soon they proved
that they could, three in the back, climbed in, closed the
doors, and he headed heavily off down the road. As he
talked to the young man beside him—also wearing sunglasses—he was conscious of three others behind him, listening. Where was his camera? In the glove compartment,
he was pretty sure, but he didn't want to check now. He was
grateful for the company but also wondered, in passing, if
they had directed him down the less desirable of the two
roads—in the direction they themselves were traveling.

Though he was not always sure he understood what his guide was saying, he carried on an amiable conversation with the young man, glancing back at the shy, pretty face of the girl in the rearview mirror. He looked at his watch—he had already been gone an hour. But then, as they wound down the narrow road, they came in sight of the sea, a wedge of blue, and at a junction they turned onto the coastal road north, and a few minutes later the man signaled for him to stop and they all got out, thanked him nicely. "Keep going straight?" he asked.

"Straight ahead, man, straight, straight."

He pulled away and followed the road as it rose and fell and wound around the leafy slope of the mountain. His back was covered with sweat now, his shirt soaked through. A warm fragrant wind swept off the sea, passed through the overheated car, and there, suddenly, was a small sign by the side of the road: "Entering the Carib Territory." Everything seemed to subtly, quietly change: the houses got smaller, for one thing, and seemed to be made differently—more of corrugated tin than wood, for example—and the first person he saw was a slight, light-skinned man with dark and wavy hair—a Carib, to be sure. He slowed down, studied the landscape with heightened attention as he bent around tighter and tighter turns, now and then passed small shops, stands really, with hand-painted signs advertising authentic crafts—baskets and beads and straw rugs.

Then he came around another turn, and there a girl was walking, a teenager, perhaps, wearing shorts and a kind of yellow fishnet top. She glanced around at the car, and he instinctively slowed down and pointed up the road. "Do you want a ride?" he asked through the open window.

"All right," said the girl and, disappointingly, she climbed into the backseat. He could see her there, in the mirror, looking out the side window. "Where are you going?" he asked, trying to be friendly.

"To Valmond."

"Where is that?"

"Straight ahead. It's a village."

"All right—tell me when we're there."

"I will," she promised. Her accent, as far as he could tell, was no different from that of others he had spoken to on the island. She too was pretty, with paler, golden-colored skin, long straight dark hair.

They drove in silence, and then came into a small settlement of houses, another shop selling crafts. "Can we stop here for a minute?" she asked softly. "I need to talk to my aunt."

"All right," Martin said, pulling over. He took off his sunglasses, put them carefully into their case, then back into his pocket. He climbed out of the car and watched as the girl walked up a path that led behind the shop; under her fishnet top she wore a halter that reached only halfway down her stomach. He stepped into a shop—empty, he thought, but then noticed that a young, silent man with a broad face was sitting in the corner and nodded when he saw him. He looked around at the things for sale—beaded necklaces, some small wicker baskets, toy bows and arrows. He bought a few necklaces, and a small straw basket to carry them in, considered buying a toy bow and arrow, but didn't. He thanked the man and then went out again into the sun, waiting for the girl but it was too hot, and he stepped into a small shop next door. It was a clean and strangely empty room: a dog slept on a bare wood floor, and an old woman stood behind the counter, silently smoking a pipe. He stood at the counter and ordered a club soda, waiting, but it was another girl who came in, younger, and also pretty, wearing an old, tired T-shirt with a faded picture of Martin Luther King. She stood by the door, leaning against the wall, and then he turned to her and asked, feigning nonchalance, "Do you know who the picture is of?"

"Of course," she said. "Martin Luther."

He waited for the last name, but when it did not come, he added "King," unable to suppress his pedagogical instincts to correct. "Martin Luther King," he repeated for emphasis, but she was not absorbing his lesson, staring distractedly across the room, and suddenly he wanted to take a picture of her, this Carib girl in a T-shirt with Martin Luther on it, and her budding breasts beneath it and her bare feet and the old grandmother smoking a pipe here in a little shop in the heart of Carib Territory. There was also the sleeping, dusty dog, the smooth, worn wood of the freshly swept floor, the sweet-smelling wind sweeping in off the sea: a sense of passing time, of waiting, but for what? People like him to show up in their rented cars and fancy sunglasses, pockets full of money and curiosity, a willingness to buy. But how to take a picture without confirming everything they suspected or knew about him already: that he was here to take things away—beads, baskets, photographs—a modern-day pirate of the Caribbean. Better to restrain himself, record this place, this moment, through other faculties, carry it back with him home. But somewhere, a clock was ticking, the hot sun was headed west, before him was a long drive back along the narrow, winding road.

It took a moment for him to speak. "Excuse me, but do you know where that girl went?" he asked the younger of the two girls, and then added in explanation, "She wanted a ride to Valmond." She smiled a sly, knowing smile, and walked silently across the floor—bare feet on wood—and called through the wall, as if she knew exactly where she was. "Rosita! Your White man wants you." The old woman chuckled; the girl with the T-shirt walked back across the room, her narrow hips swinging. A moment later Rosita bounded down into the room through another door. Something about her had changed—her hair, lipstick?

"Okay," she said, "I'm ready." Her sister smiled, and Rosita gave her a mock slap on the way out.

"Thank you," Martin said, turning back to the old woman and the girl. The woman nodded, the girl smiled again.

Although he had left all the windows open the car was hotter still. "You can sit in the front, if you want," he proposed, and she did. He pulled his sunglasses out of his pocket again, took them out of the fancy case, and put them on. He started the car and drove off, plotting his next attempt at conversation. As he shifted through the gears he was aware of the smooth skin of Rosita's bare thighs beside him, bathed in sunlight, sliding upward under the frayed hem of her jeans. "It's a nice name—Rosita," he said.

She nodded, and said, "Thank you."

"How do you like my sunglasses?" he asked foolishly, turning toward her so she could see them better.

"They're all right," she said, unenthusiastically. He wanted to tell her the whole story—how they had been given to him by a friend, a beautiful Danish woman with a constellation of freckles on her cheeks and across the smooth skin above her breasts, and a way of uttering the word "pleasure" that caused him, for the first time in his life, to understand what it really meant. But she was far away now, back in her native country, or maybe back in her little village with her parents, strolling down the streets of Copenhagen. But it all was hopeless anyway—she was married, for one thing, as was he, with a lovely wife and a beautiful daughter, faithfully waiting for him back in America. He had never really had an affair before, didn't really know how to do it, and looked back on this one, now, with a peculiar mixture of pride and regret; he felt vaguely guilty, but happy also, and what, anyway, could he have done? A summer month away, a warm and pleasant climate, classes in the day, free time at night; within a week or so, their fellow conferees had formed themselves into little social clusters, and they had gravitated toward each other, and whatever emotional resources one is supposed to summon at such moments, the ability to say "Ah, this is all very lovely, but . . ." he discovered he lacked entirely. She was beautiful, besides, and laughed a lot, lived only two doors away from him in the large and lonely dormitory, and, unlike most people he knew, did not consider adultery much of a sin, much less a crime. "Americans take things so seriously," she said. One must live! In another thirty or forty years, they would all be dead, anyway, dust, the earth spinning along on its axis, their time spent together one summer month of a long lost year nearly forgotten, if not forgiven.

"A friend gave them to me," he said to Rosita, simplifying. And then he asked, changing the subject, "Where are you from?"

"Here," she said. "But I live in Roseau."

"And you came to visit?"

"To see my daughter. She lives with my mother."

A daughter? Another bubble burst! She was only sixteen or so—a virgin, he had imagined.

"And how old is your daughter?"

"Going on two," she said, and then said quickly, pointing up the road, "It's here, by the tree."

He slowed down, but before he came to a complete stop he blurted out the question that had been festering in him. "Do you mind if I take your picture? I'm a teacher, and I'd like to show my students and—"

"It's all right," she said, as if she had heard all this before—a photograph of the pretty Carib girl. They climbed out and he got his camera, suddenly nervous, and she drifted over toward a tree that bore a pretty reddish flower.

"Where?" she asked shyly.

"That's fine," he said, and raised the camera to his eye, but it clunked against something—glass. He took off the sunglasses and, for lack of a better place, put them on the hood of the car. Then Rosita smiled shyly, prettily; he took one picture, said "Wait," and then took another. "Very nice. Thank you. If you give me your address I can send you one."

She shrugged. "All right." She had heard this before too—the getting of the address to send a letter that would never come, just another thing to hold on to. He fumbled in his wallet for a scrap of paper, and then went back to the steaming car for a pencil, and she wrote her name and address in a perfect, elegant script—Rosita Valmond, Valmond, Carib Territory, Dominica. He gave her his card, issued by his school.

"I'll send it to you," he said. "But it may take a few weeks. Don't worry."

"That's okay," she said, and with no further formalities she turned and walked down the road—a pretty teenage girl in cutoff shorts and a yellow fishnet top. She, too, he would never see again—but she was in his camera now, in miniature, captured in silver, upside down on the film. Quietly triumphant, he climbed back into the car, started it up, turned around, and then headed slowly back down the road in the direction from which he had come, taking in his final impressions of this place—the heat, the sweet-smelling wind, a sense of waiting, time standing still. It was only two o'clock—still time to stop at the emerald pool on his way home, or the small scruffy beach on the edge of town. He would send her the picture—they would correspond.

Outside, the passing world was green and beautiful, and to his left were glimpses of the sea. But why was everything so bright? He slapped his forehead, his squinting eyes, but there was nothing there. He reached for his pockets—also nothing—and then skidded to a halt on the road's crumbling verge. He searched madly in the car—pockets, under the seat, glove compartment, where he found the fine leather case—empty. Pockets again, then he cursed loudly, then turned the car around, speeding back into the Carib Territory.

The photograph: the camera knocking against his glasses . . . he had put them onto the hood of the car, and in his fumbling efforts to take her picture and get her address, forgotten them there, and driven off without them. He had broken into a sudden panicky sweat, and he was driving too fast now, his third time down the road that day.

"Jesus Christ!!" he cursed, scanning the road for signs of the sunglasses—a fragment, even, a clue, a piece of broken glass—but there was nothing. Had they survived the fall? And then he came around the final bend, and saw the tree with its beautiful red flowers, but there was nothing on the road, nothing where they should have been. A few minutes before, they both had been there, taking the photograph—she standing by the tree, he taking the picture, the sunglasses on the hot hood of the car—but that was the past; this was the present. Now he was alone on the curve of the road. He stopped and leaped out and looked for his own tire tracks, or footprints of the girl, and tried to reconstruct the physics of departure—had he gone forward or backward, for example. A small boy appeared, pushing a rattling metal wheel along with a bent piece of wire, and looked up when he saw him. "Sunglasses," Martin explained. "They fell off the car when I drove away. Have you seen any?" The boy, with wavy dark hair, stared blankly back at him, and then shook his head no, sorry to disappoint.

He stalked up the road, retracing the path of the car, and tried to imagine their fate—bouncing along in the weeds, or crushed under another car's wheels—but there was no sign of broken glass, nor bent and mangled metal—airplane alloy. More likely, they were picked up by the first pedestrian who came along—a shambling Rasta-Carib. He returned to the car and rummaged frantically under the seats, in the back, and there, maddeningly, found a pair of sunglasses stuffed between the cushions. But they were not his: they were old and cheap, with scratched plastic lenses. "Shit," he said, but threw them onto the front seat anyway—he would keep them to barter with. He went back to the tree and studied the dust for clues. Should he go look for Rosita? Should he start knocking on doors, and ask if anyone had found them? Too embarrassing—the sweating White man groveling for a pair of sunglasses. Maybe he could find an identical pair back in America. Not likely. Or maybe Rosita herself had found them? He would write her and ask, and offer a one-hundred-dollar reward, and she could ask around, and mail them to him when she found them. Ridiculous; better to get out of here, accept the loss, like other people did, admit that they, and the woman who had given them to him, and the time they had shared, were gone forever.

He jumped into the car and sped a hundred yards down the road, and then went back the other way, scanning the verges of the road. Nothing. He glanced again at the seat, saw the old, crappy sunglasses, grabbed at them and flung them out the window, could hear them as they went crashing through the leaves—more sunglasses for the Caribs! He tried to calm himself down and drive more slowly. The car wound through the scattered houses, the hot wind and sun baking him now, his shirt sodden with sweat. He needed water. He passed the sign that welcomed him to Carib Territory, read it in the rearview mirror.

At the junction of the road that turned up the mountain there was a young boy in the shadow of a single palm tree who held out his arm as he approached, and he stopped to offer him a ride. He needed company to help calm him down. The boy climbed into the back and answered his questions in monosyllables—yes sir, no sir—and then sat in silence, a sullen witness to his unhappiness.

His attempts at conversation did not help, and as he drove back toward his dismal guesthouse, with its bare bulb and creaking bed, his mood darkened and then congealed, settling in for good. He tried to extract some consolation from his sad adventure, elicit some humor or wisdom from the layers of ironies which, as an afterglow from the conference, now offered themselves up to him for study. How had it happened?

It was the photograph, clearly, that was the seed of his misfortune: the sunglasses had been taken from him as the price of the picture, as compensation for his peculiar need to take it, steal the girl's soul and beauty and smuggle them back to America. "How do you like my sunglasses?" he had asked in the car, and the whole sad story emanated from this one pitiful moment of vanity—bolstered by his recent adventures. (He was forty years old.) If he had simply let her out and said good-bye, released her to her world and watched her walk away down the sunstruck road through the warm wind, the sunglasses would still be there, resting lightly on his face, diffusing the world in their cool, dispassionate light.

On the other hand, it had been his kindly impulse to get her address, to send her the picture, that had really caused him to forget them, leave them on the hood of the car and drive off, hadn't it? Or perhaps the getting of her address was born of some less noble impulse, something less to do with kindliness and more to do with her cutoff jeans, her yellow fishnet top, the diamond patterns of shadow it cast on her bare, smooth belly, her sun-warmed thighs on the seat beside him? Why not leave well enough alone, let their few shared moments moving across the arc of the earth be what it was? Always needing something else to preserve or validate the encounter. "Don't lose them," Sophie had said hopefully when she had given them, shyly, and he could picture her soft blue eyes, the constellation of freckles on her high cheeks as she sat above him on the bed, smiling down. Now, in spite of or because of his acute desire not to, he had lost them anyway, an unnecessary reminder that their time together was finished too, added to the scrap heap of history.

The fancy leather case lay on the seat behind him, empty, taunting him with its golden script. What to do with it now? Throw it out the window too? No, he would have to keep it as a bittersweet memento of his loss, keep it closed, holding in the warm, sweet-scented air of the Carib Territory, smelling vaguely of smoke and sweat, blood and salt, sugar and rum—and with it the monstrous history of the Americas. He could retrieve the fragrance whenever he wanted, open the case and breathe it in, careful not to let it all escape. Even the sunglasses he could recover in memory, and slip them into one of his dry meditations on history, never to be published.

"It's here," a small voice behind him said, startling him. "At this tree." He had almost forgotten the boy, his passenger captive, and when he pulled over he turned to look back at him—a soft, beautiful face, deep brown skin, long, almost feminine eyelashes.

"Thank you, sir."

"You're welcome." Martin wanted to say something more, but what? He could think of nothing. Instead, he watched as the boy walked away—bare feet, tattered shorts, smooth, strong legs. A truck roared past. He resumed his climb up the mountain, but missed the boy's presence, there in the backseat, more than he would have imagined. He was sorry to be again alone.

And then they returned: he could picture the sunglasses as they rested happily on the face of their new owner—an old woman smoking a pipe, or a slight, skipping girl laughing her way along a dappled, sunlit path, singing in her sweet West Indian voice. No: they now resided, he felt certain, on the face of a rakish young man who would use them to impress and seduce women, maybe even Rosita herself. He chuckled unhappily at the thought, and worried, too, that the new owner would not fully appreciate the beauty and value of his new acquisition, and never know that they had been meticulously and lovingly created by highly skilled craftsmen in the land that had given birth, half a millennium or so before, to a small, inquisitive boy named Cristoforo Colombo.

Love Songs from America

Small sounds—a singing bird, a shuffling cow, the squawk and scrabble of chickens as they peck and scratch around the kitchen door. A dog barks, and I can hear the soft laughter of people walking along the path that runs along the edge of the neighbor's fields, and then catch a glimpse of them—a flash of color, a half-turned face—through the leaves. From the other side of the house I hear the muffled sound of voices as Njoki and her mother sit and work in the courtyard between the house and the kitchen: boiling the hard, yellow maize, pulling the kernels off the cob, cooking it some more in a large clay pot over a wooden fire in the kitchen—a small stone structure that sits beside the house. But the chimney doesn't quite work, and the dark room is always filled with smoke, billowing in the pale light that filters in through the doorway.

Although Njoki and her siblings have pitched in to buy their parents a small gas stove, when it runs out of gas there seems to be neither the money nor the will to replace it. When Njoki chides her mother for this, she just smiles, and says, in English, "Ah, we're just used to the old ways," and then laughs, by way of explanation, and adds, "We're old."

"In your thinking," Njoki adds, but her mother—a mother of twelve children—doesn't seem to hear her.

Now and then I hear the voice of the boy, Harold, as he drifts around the place, visiting the animals he has befriended in the few hours since we have arrived—a scrawny cat, a dog that has just given birth to two puppies, the goats that live in a pen behind the house. There is the sound of the wind in the trees, and lowing of the two cows, the voice of Wairimū, the house girl, chopping wood, softly singing to herself as she works. Once or twice a day there is also the sound of a plane passing overheard—the old-fashioned, wavering growl of propellers churning the air, like old movies of World War II, and I am reminded then of my own mother, seven or eight or nine thousand miles away, a third of the way around the world, worrying. She doesn't like airplanes much, doesn't like, she told me a day or two before we left, "people I love flying around in them."

When we arrived in London after a fitful all-night flight from America, we made our way by the underground to a vast and beautiful park, and all lay down on the well-clipped English lawn, taking warmth from the sun that had just risen above the trees. I must have fallen asleep, and when I finally woke, Njoki was lying nearby, sound asleep in the sun, but where was the boy? I leaped up, and there, twenty feet off, he was playing by himself in the shadow of a small tree, trying to climb up into its lower branches.

"Harold!" I said, startled by the sight of him alone in the middle of a park of a foreign city.

"Just playing," he said happily, wondering what he had done wrong, and I sat back down on the grass in a hazy stupor. How long had he been there, wandering around by himself, as his tired parents slept?

We spent the day camped out in the sun, taking occasional walks to a small lake to look at the geese and watch tourists paddle around in aluminum boats, and it was only later, toward midafternoon, that we headed back toward the tube and the airport, for our second night aloft. That's when I saw the large headlines, at the newspaper stand: "Plane Crashes into Sea off New York. 230 Feared Dead."

"Shit," I heard myself mutter, but kept it to myself, and when we got to the airport, I snuck into a shop to skim the article: a 747 bound for Paris crashed into the Long Island Sound twelve minutes out of Kennedy, its fragments and passengers now washing up along the southern beaches of Long Island. The plane had left America only a couple hours after we did, and it occurs to me we were airborne, high over Newfoundland, when it crashed. The boy was splayed out on the seats, asleep, when I got back to the lounge.

"Jesus," I said to Njoki. "It just blew up for no reason—a 747, like the one we're about to get on. My mother is probably hysterical."

"But she knows it's not *our* plane."

"I know, but still—the same night we leave? We were in the air when it blew up."

By the time we take off the second time he has fallen asleep again, and I hold his hand as we go throttling down the runway, and then with a sudden, hopeful lurch, bound up into the air, the plane wheeling high above the flickering lights of England, over the blue-black channel, and then heading south over France, the Mediterranean, North Africa, and I look down at his beautiful face lit by the flickering light from the wing outside. And soon, drinks are on the way—a half carafe of wine, and little bags of peanuts, and all seems well and cozy in the great, trembling mass of metal we are riding in, floating over the varied troubles of this earth—war, famine, pestilence, genocide, drought. But we are high above it now, a few hundred groggy souls passing in and out of sleep, sedated by wine. I, too, fall into a thin sleep, and the next time I look the sky is pale in the east, and the boy is awake beside me, nattering happily and going over the components of his breakfast. "Look, Dad, eggs," he says, and soon we are on our way down again, as light as a feather, rising and falling on the high equatorial winds.

"We have seven acres here," Njoki's father is telling us as we walk along the path, his hand gesturing toward the slope of land that tilts up and rises past the small cow barn. "We grow maize, beans, pumpkin. This is an avocado tree, mango, banana." Harold is running along before us, excited by the novelties of farm life, by the big, musty presence of cows and goats, the small white rabbits he discovered in a cage behind the house. "And here is coffee." He points to the rows and rows of the small, innocuous trees bearing the small green berries. "But prices are very low now. Very low. So we are not concentrating much on that."

The boy is running, still, and I half worry he will run into a piece of barbed wire as I did, on our first visit here, before he was born. The path loops around through the coffee trees and soon we are back at the house, looking at the two sweet-smelling cows, one of which, I am told, was bought with two hundred dollars I sent—a token effort I made to live up to my expectations as a son-in-law. I am aware that because I am of another culture and country, I have partially shirked my obligations as a son-in-law, but Njoki assures me that this is not so, that her family is grateful for whatever I can give, and the cow has borne a calf, a pretty light brown animal which is grazing in the yard, tethered to a stake.

Harold is anxious to see the outhouse, of which he has been informed but which he has not yet seen. He runs up to the house for his flashlight, and we peer down through the teardrop hole in the stone platform into the fetid, swampy depths, twenty feet below. "Cool," he reports, and wants to know who dug the hole. "The workman, probably," I say, "a long time ago." He tries it out—takes a pee while I hold the light, listening for the delayed sound when it reaches bottom. Satisfied, we head out, and he is off, running again, and I hear him say, "I'm going to go see the goats."

I had wanted a girl. When I found out it was a boy, inadvertently, two months before he was born, I walked around the city for a couple of hours in a haze of incredulity—something about the strange silences that fall between fathers and sons, affection smothered beneath our embarrassed maleness, love that has trouble finding a way out. Or perhaps I just thought it would be more interesting having a child of another gender, witnessing this miraculous and mysterious transformation of baby to girl to a woman. Whatever uncertainties that remained disappeared, of course, at birth, evaporated in his actual presence, a day or two old, blinking the world slowly into focus. Harold, we named him, after my father's father, with a middle name Kamau, after Njoki's father. And who could have told me of the quiet, crushing love of a parent, silent ache of longing one feels, even in the presence of the child, and the smoldering determination, in spite of one's own inadequacies, to protect him from the perils of this world?

Now, six years later, Njoki has not gotten pregnant since, and it seems likely that he will be an only child. And in this, he will unwittingly keep alive a family tradition, of sorts, a lineage of only children: my father, my father's mother, her husband's father. Bereft of siblings, he will be rich in cousins, and part of our coming here is for this, to see the side of the family he has caught only glimpses of, through photographs back in America.

When we first arrived after our two nights of flying we stayed for a few days at Njoki's sister's house in an affluent suburb of Nairobi, five or six fenced acres of lawn, trees, and bushes. Here, he fell happily in with his cousins—two older girls, two younger boys—and spent a couple days playing with them, riding a bicycle on the grass, taunting the three geese who walked around like sentries, playing with the small soccer ball that we brought with us from home. He had worried about fitting in, about being different—of lighter skin, with straighter hair, with a different accent— and so it was partly through the force of his own will, the desire to be like his cousins, that in the day or two after our arrival, his voice already began to change—assume the lilt and cadences and rolling *r*'s of his cousins. At first I thought it was a conscious imitation, but when I suggested he was making fun of them he turned, incredulous, and said, rolling his *r*, "But, Dad—I'm not even trying!" Against my better judgment I have found the change unsettling, as if in some strange and subtle way he is becoming someone slightly other than the boy I know.

In the evening the darkness comes quickly, and we eat dinner in the orange glow of gas lanterns, drink hot milk fresh from the cow, warmed over the fire and then poured into a thermos. In the morning, after a fitful night's sleep in a room so dark I cannot find the door, I step out into the milky, ash gray light of morning. It is July, the cold season here, the cool weather moving up from the south, and though it has not yet rained the sun has not shown either, only burned through the clouds, as a pale, drifting coin in the late afternoon. Njoki's parents are away at church, and when they return her father has brought me a present of the morning's paper, news of the world beyond the ridges and valleys and small farms of Kikuyuland: first the local politics, and then the rest of Africa—a photograph of a crash of two *matatus*, minibuses, in Nyeri, that has killed twenty-three people.

On page 5 or so, some news of America—a flood in Ohio, a few children dug up in someone's backyard, the president speaking out against domestic violence. And then I stumble onto what I am looking for, the plane: a few life preservers floating around in the ocean, a great orange fireball over the Long Island Sound, the ocean floor littered with parts and fragments of the plane and of people who, a few minutes before, had been unbuckling their seat belts and glancing over their shoulder for the stewardess, bathed in perfume, bearing gifts. What does it feel like when your plane starts to "break apart" in midair, and the wind comes in, and the starlight, and the peanuts and wineglasses fall, and you clutch your child's hand and tell him, by way of apology, that you love him, and he's a good boy, as you descend, a small family of three, through the high, chilly atmosphere, the waning light of an otherwise lovely summer's evening?

But we are close to the earth here, happily—the rust red earth that stains the hems of our pants, the hands of the boy, and the soles of my shoes, the feet of the chickens who drift around in the courtyard, squawking and scratching and waiting for scraps of food that may fall their way, the nightly scattering of maize. There is the scrawny dog who has just given birth to two puppies; one is healthy and happy and stumbles around; the other is small and sickly with phlegmy eyes, and sleeps much of the time, the mother lying beside her. It is the sick dog that Harold is drawn to, and wants to pet, though he was encouraged not to. "Is he going to die?" he keeps asking, and when he is told "Probably," he responds less with sadness than with curiosity. "When?" he wants to know, as if afraid he might miss it.

But the day passes slowly, if not for him, then for me. I suffer from a mild case of claustrophobia, or agoraphobia, and after a couple of days the countryside seems to close in around me, and evokes some of the same sensations I felt, once, visiting my own grandparents' farm, back in Pennsylvania—the same shimmering scents of hay and manure and hot fields, the same interwoven lives of animals and people. But my grandmother died a month before Harold was born, and so they never met, but I inherited her car, a Buick Skylark which still held in its soft seats the fragrance of the farm, and for his first year he spent driving around, asleep, mostly, but taking into his new lungs the pleasant musty odor of Pennsylvania, of hay and animals and people, of his ancestors, now gone. In those days, I used to keep the windows rolled up to hold it all in, like an archaeologist of the air, preserving this last, ephemeral inheritance of the past.

I sit and read, and write a letter or two, and drift back into the house, where I find him, sitting on the couch in the weak light that finds its way through the window. He has a small tape player on his lap, and is listening to a song he has brought with him from home. He has fallen in love, this spring, with Mariah Carey, and does not stop singing when he sees me, as he once did, but continues on, open faced and unembarrassed, at ease with his adoration. And the song I am hearing is a beautiful one, and I catch fragments:

> *But the time went sailing by*
> *Reluctantly we said goodbye . . .*

The song is a sad, sweet river he is floating on—and hearing it I half fall in love with Mariah Carey myself, and I am fearful in advance for the heartache he may suffer at the hands of women, capable both of great love and neglect. Maybe he will be stronger than I was, or smarter, less susceptible to the allure of love and lust and beauty, and I leave him there, in the half-light that comes in through the window, singing these melancholy love songs from America.

Toward evening we kick a ball around for a while in the front yard, and then I coax him into taking a short walk with me on the narrow road of packed rust red earth. But he is shy, and doesn't like being stared at, especially by children. I don't like being stared at either, and part of my asking him to come is so that I will have company, will have a context, and reluctantly he agrees. But there are few people out on the road—an old woman stooped beneath an enormous bundle of sticks, a man on an ancient, creaking bicycle, weaving along the road, an elderly man, drunk and with crooked yellow teeth, who insists on shaking my hand, and won't let go, talking in Kikuyu. Harold observes all this calmly, and when the grinning man finally lets go of my hand, he says softly, "What did he want?"

"To say hello."

"Why did it take so long?"

"He got stung by bees."

"He did?"

"Not really. He's drunk, Harold. That's what they say here when you drink too much—that you were stung by bees."

"Oh," he says, mulling it over. "I think he needs to go to the dentist."

The road bends to the right, revealing itself beyond, and I can see a group of children trickling out of the school yard, the beginning of a torrent that will soon follow. Before we have time to turn around they have already seen us, and I can hear their shouts and cries following us up the road. "Uh-oh," I say.

"What?" he wants to know.

"Some kids are coming."

"So?" he says defiantly, though I can tell that he, too, is less than thrilled.

"Anyway, we've walked far enough." We turn and drift back toward the house, but before we get there we hear the patter of bare feet behind us, murmuring of voices, and I turn and look and there are a dozen or so children coming up behind us to get a closer look. With the only phrase of Kikuyu I know, I say, "Mũrĩ ega."

They look surprised, and a few of them say "Nĩ kwega"

back. They are cute, this entourage, the stuff of *National Geographic* photographs with their tired uniforms of varying shades of blue. We continue walking, and they get closer, and I glance down at Harold in time to see him turn back to them and stick out his tongue.

"Harold!" I say, surprised but amused. "Don't do that."

"They started it!" he protests. "I saw them."

"They did?" I ask, and then add, pointlessly, "They wouldn't."

"They did too!" he says, and I can tell by his tone that he feels wronged, first by them, and then me. We have reached the path to the house, and I turn to the group of kids, who stop suddenly, and wave. "Good-bye," they say stiffly.

"How are you?" one of them asks, trying out his English.

"Fine, how are you?" I say, but I have exhausted their repertoire, and I am no better in Kikuyu. I repeat my one phrase of greeting, wondering if it will also pass for good-bye.

"Nĩ kwega," they say, and suddenly run away, laughing and shouting, triumphant after their encounter.

"See, they're just shy," I say.

He has taken his thumb into his mouth, a sign he has turned inward, brooding.

"Stupid kids," he says.

That evening we are to have chicken for supper, and in the waning light Njoki's mother has snatched up a handsome, plump hen from the yard, and is carrying it around with her like an anxious handbag as it squawks and stares around it with wild, bewildered eyes.

"That's the one?" Harold wants to know, and follows her into the dark kitchen, where a great pot of water is boiling over a wood fire, the long, thin logs projecting out onto the stone floor, pushed into the fire as they burn out. And it is there, his face glowing in the yellow light, his grandmother murmuring soft, amused words of comfort to the struggling bird, that she slits its throat with a strangely affectionate gesture of knife and hand, an unexpected, searing sound, and lets the blood drain into a cup, like she is pouring a pitcher of milk, the dead bird's feet twitching out the last electrical impulses of life. I've seen enough, and step out into the darkness, but the boy stays on to watch the rest, excited by the ritual—the chicken doused in the boiling pot, feathers torn out, and then its body disemboweled and divvied up for cooking. Afterward, Harold seems strangely elated by this drama of death he has witnessed, and leaps around in the gloaming. Later, as we eat the tough country bird in the yellow pools of kerosene lamps, he seems untroubled by the memory of the animal we are eating, strutting about the yard, and when I try to tease him about it he says, "So? The ones we eat at home were living too."

I sleep badly. The night is too long and too dark, and I am dreaming too vividly of home—some confusing jumble about playing golf with my father and some of his friends, only not being able to find my ball in the rough and everyone waiting, then finally giving up on me and heading off into the distance, me dropping another ball, hitting it badly, and then rushing, and then there is that old, underwater feeling, of quicksand, of not being able to move fast enough to catch up. And then, in the utter darkness, I wonder what my son's memories of this place will be, and recall that I was his age when I gathered my first impressions of my own grandfather, for whom he was named: a large, gentle man who moved through the world with a slow, mysterious grace, befriending random people on street corners and in checkout lines and parking lots. One time I drove into a hot Pennsylvania city with him on some long-forgotten errand: I remember the heat and the glint of sunlight on railroad tracks, and the easy weight of him, in rolled-up shirtsleeves, as he moved through the humid swelter of America. I get up now, and in the dim light I see the outline of the boy in the adjacent bed. I straighten out his covers, and go back to my musty bed that makes my back ache, and will myself to sleep until dawn.

The morning is a sunny one, and as I lie in bed I can hear the corrugated tin of the roof creaking and groaning as it expands and contracts in the sunlight and shadows cast by passing clouds. From the kitchen, I hear the happy voice of the child, nattering away with his grandparents, discussing the recently departed chicken. He wants to know, it seems, where the one we ate had come from, and the best his grandmother can come up with is "an egg," but he then wants to know which chicken laid that egg and what happened to her. "Ahh," I hear her say with a resigned laugh, "we must have eaten that one, too."

I pull on my clothes and drift outside, and rather than walk to the outhouse I pee under a bush beside the house, hoping no visitors wander into the yard. That would be news in the village—the *Mzungu* peeing under a bush at Kamau's house—but no one does. Afterward, as I sit in the kitchen yard in the sunlight, my father-in-law returns from church with the morning paper, where, happily, I find no news of the plane—no people falling out of the sky.

Later, in an effort to stave off my gathering restlessness, I try to make myself useful and take upon myself the task of chopping wood for the cooking fire. The logs are not the clunky American kind that cleave into two under the lusty blow of an ax, but are long and sinewy and require a more delicate, accurate blow, and then need to be levered apart with a subtle sideways motion of the ax I find difficult to master. Harold watches me, waiting for his turn, and lies down on the grass nearby. This seems like a bad idea, somehow, but I am not quite sure why, and a moment later he leaps up, furiously scratching. I look down at the ground where he has been and there is a long, sinuous trail of ants where he lay—"fire ants" of a kind that, I have been told, once they discover you swarm over your body, biting. "They can kill you," Njoki had warned. I take off his shirt, find the one that bit him and look for others, but there are none. He is still scratching himself, and as I take him into the house for his mother to check for more, I hear him whimper, almost to himself, "I want to go home." Why, I wonder, am I almost happy to hear this?

Later we go to lunch, but, not wanting to subject himself to the attentions of the children of the village, he asks to stay behind on the *shamba* with his grandparents. It feels odd to leave him, to be walking along the road without him, but when I tell this to Njoki she says, "I think it's wonderful he's comfortable enough to stay with his grandparents."

"I didn't say it wasn't wonderful," I say, unnecessarily. "I said it felt weird."

The walk is farther than I had imagined—a mile or so along the narrow road of bumpy red earth, clay almost; we pause now and then to talk to family friends who have heard of our visit; when we reach the village—a motley collection of tired-looking buildings, and a few old women selling vegetables in the shade of a large tree—we turn left, drop down to the river and rise up again, and turn into the pathway to the house. Lunch is pleasant enough, but after a few formalities and introductions the conversation drifts into Kikuyu and I am left to listen, catching a word of English now and then, or being told by Njoki what they are talking about. Outside, I walk around the yard and exchange a few words with the house girl, but her English is limited too, and I miss the company of the boy, Harold, who serves as a kind of intermediary between me and this place— someone, when all else fails, to talk to. I am more than ready to head back to the house when Njoki emerges, full of laughter; I take a couple photographs of her with her aunt, and we start back along the road.

"That was fun," she says. "She's always been my favorite aunt. She only wished we had brought Harold."

"Why didn't we?"

"He didn't want to come, remember? In any case, it's good for my parents—they need to spend time with him too."

"Did she ask you when we're going to have another one, like everyone else?"

"Oh, no; she just told me to be grateful for the one we have. She said, 'Some women have only one egg.'"

Along the road I lighten and try to stop grousing; it's a beautiful day, and a warm yellow light filters down through the leaves and lies dappled along the road. Some pretty girls from the high school are walking along in front of us, their blue uniforms altered to absorb their swelling women's bodies—I can see the expanded stitch, a darker thread in the faded cloth, let out to absorb their hips and breasts, and now and then they sneak a look back at us. Njoki, it occurs to me, was one of them not so long ago—the smartest girl in her class, walking this narrow road of packed earth that led her away, first to the city, Nairobi, and then across the ocean to America. We say hello, and a couple of them stop and shyly shake our hands, and then run off laughing. "Silly girls," she says. "I know their mother. She's my age."

I am eager to get back to the house: what if something happened—he ran into a barbed-wire fence or got bit by a goat? No phone to call the doctor, no car to drive him there, and a mile to walk to the main road. I have always felt somewhat uneasy in Africa, intimidated by the great, yawning vastness of the place—the continent stretching away in all directions, beyond imagining. Life feels more tenuous, and death closer at hand—road accidents, a swarm of ants, the bite of the wrong mosquito, and then a day or two delay to the doctor, the city too far, no transport, no phone, cries and wails in the village, and then the rust red earth, waiting to take us in. When her grandfather was buried, Njoki told me, he was not placed in a coffin, but by tradition wrapped in a simple shroud, covered with leaves, and then a blanket of soil in the shade of an old mango tree. "Then," her mother has said, only half joking, "the ants can begin their work."

All is well back at the house, and I find Harold sitting happily with his grandmother, pulling the kernels off a husk of corn, tossing a few to the chickens who swarm at his feet.

"Mom, Dad," he says when he sees us. "You know that puppy, the sick one?"

"Yeah?"

"Well," he says, pausing, breaking the news to us gently, "he died."

"He did?"

"Yeah." He is thrilled by this pageant of life and death, the bracing reality of it all. "Guka buried him already. Want to go see the grave?"

"No thanks," I say. "Maybe tomorrow." I settle for the living rabbits instead, and I follow him behind the house to two beautiful white babies who live in a cage five or six feet off the ground so the dogs won't get them. He pulls one out by the ears, and then cradles it in his arms, like a baby.

"Can we get one when we get home?"

"We'll see."

With every passing year, it seems less and less likely that a sibling will be forthcoming, heightening my already over-active sense of nostalgia. A child moves out into the world in a series of small steps, subtle milestones that often pass unnoticed. Although I was grateful the day he learned how to swing without my help, "pumping" with his two legs, there was a sadness that this simple and wearying task of parenthood—hours pushing behind the swing—was no lon-ger required. And there was another moment of illumination the first time I heard, lying half awake in the blue-gray dawn, the sound of his feet walking—not to our bed, as he always had, but to the bathroom, and then the sound of him peeing, and then his feet carrying him back to his own bed. He has gotten too heavy to carry, almost, but when he falls asleep on the couch at home, I cling to the ritual of carrying him up to bed—preferring the risk of dropping him to relinquishing this task of fatherhood, and I stagger up the last few steps of our narrow staircase under his gathering weight, barely making it across the room before laying him heavily down.

From the rabbits he has drifted away, again, in search of adventure, and I follow the trail of his murmured love songs back behind the buildings to a tree into which he has climbed. It is an avocado, and its fruit, not yet ripe, hangs in the branches with the pendulous weight of breasts. I walk in under its blue shadow and find him there, standing on a branch a few feet off the ground, looking down at me with a sly, bemused expression, wondering if I am going to order him down. No, boys need to climb trees, test their limits, and to his surprise I encourage him to climb higher if he wants to—farther out, holding on to the branch above him as he goes. "Higher?" he asks, looking down at me.

"If you want to. Just hold on, that's all . . . and watch where you step." He inches up along the branch, glancing back at me now and then for affirmation, and when he gets to another fork, a foot or two higher than I am tall, he stops.

"Okay, that's high enough." I say, but then I can't help myself, and lightly shake the branch from below.

"Windy," I say as the leaves shake and tremble, the avocados swaying around him. "Windy!"

"No, Daddy, no," he pleads, clutching the branch, and I stop. And then he just stands there for a minute, surveying the scene from above, enjoying the view.

"Okay, now, come down."

He pauses for a moment, looking down, and then starts along the branch with small, careful steps. But I must have glanced away for a second, and one of his feet must have slipped, or the branch he was holding on to broke off, for the next thing I know he has shifted in midair, suddenly and without warning, and before I have a chance to react or reach out, he is on the descent—not in slow motion like they say it's going to be, but all of a sudden and in a blur—a boy falling to earth, his hands reaching out into thin air, his small chest thumping off one branch, his body flipping around as he drops the rest of the way—less a boy, suddenly, than a weight, a bag of sand or wheat, inanimate and helpless, at the mercy of gravity. There is no time even to respond, to catch him, only to reach toward him in a lame gesture of helplessness before he lands with a sickening thump on the ground, among the dry leaves and rotting fruit and sticks and scattered stones.

I cry out—a strange inarticulate sound from some unfamiliar part of me—and rush down to him and pick him up quickly, as if to undo what has just happened. His arms wrap themselves around my neck and cling in a sudden, fierce grip of fear. "Jesus, are you all right?" I say, convinced that something must be broken—his arm, or rib, or leg.

"Does anything hurt?" I ask, but he is sobbing now, breathless less from landing than from shock, and I walk around rubbing his back, jostling him back to life. "Are you okay?" I keep asking, and he keeps holding me, and then lets out a single syllable between the breaths, "Yeah."

I set him down gently, like a cracked vase, to inspect for damage—a scrape on his arm and ribs, a tear in his new shirt from the branch, a leaf in his hair—but he reports no other pains. "Does it feel like anything is broken?" I ask, and he shakes his head, his cheeks flushed and traced with tears. Together, we look up at the branch from which he has fallen, a foot or two higher than I am tall—too high, it now seems obvious, for a boy of six to be climbing.

"Stupid tree," he says.

"It's not the tree's fault," I say, failing to offer another possibility. Instead, I wipe the tears away and straighten out his shirt, and brush off a fleck of squashed avocado. I find a small, broken branch on the ground and speculate that he grabbed on to it, and it broke, causing his descent. He shakes his head again, no, and I pick him up and carry him out from under the tree, twigs snapping underfoot, wondering how I will report his misadventure to his mother and grandparents.

He is still taking in air in short little gasps but is coming back to his old self, gaining distance on his mishap. "Dad," he says softly, sensing in me a need for clarity, closure—an explanation we can both agree upon. "I think I know what made me fall."

"What?" I ask warily, bracing myself: I know that something is coming, but I don't know what it is. He pauses before answering, in a voice at once soft and clear, weighted with a secret meaning. "It was the wind."

Adjunct

On the first night of class, Robert did not notice among the unfamiliar faces any which evoked in him that little spark of recognition he sometimes felt as a teacher—that illicit spark of attraction that lent to the class a certain romantic undertone and, if nothing else, made the term go faster. Instead, it was all a kind of blur: seventeen wary faces staring dully back at him as he went through the slow litany of requirements and expectations—"If you have more than three unexcused absences, your grade will diminish at the rate of . . ."—and his unconvincing attempts to sound like a "hard" teacher. As he spoke, he could feel the class growing restless, listing toward the door like flowers toward the light. "Are there any questions?" he asked, scanning the room, and could feel himself giving way to their collective expectation to get out early. "No? Well, in that case," he said, pausing for effect, "I guess you can all leave—go buy the books, perhaps."

There followed a collective sigh of relief, rustling of books and papers and autumn coats and sweaters, shuffling of shoes on linoleum and a few scattered "Good nights" as the room emptied itself and the students filed out into the night.

It was only then that she came in—a breathless young woman clutching in her hand a slip of pink paper, and wearing in her hair a translucent barrette of matching pink.

"Is this, ah . . . English 101?" she said, catching her breath, holding her hand to her chest; in her voice Robert thought he heard the lilting cadence of the Caribbean.

"Yes" he said, looking away from her beautiful, open face and almond eyes, back toward his desk, slowly gathering his papers and stuffing them into his floppy canvas briefcase. "Is that the course you want?"

"I think so." She held out for him the square of pink.

"English 101 . . . Tuesday night, six o'clock to nine . . . Robert Walters . . . that's me, I guess." He took from his briefcase a syllabus and handed it to her, and then watched her as she read it—her high, smooth forehead the color of cocoa, her handsome squarish jaw, the few wisps of hair that had escaped her barrette and rose in a kind of kinetic frenzy above her face.

"Is there any homework?" she asked.

"Not really," Robert said, looking up at her. "Just buy the two books and come to class next time."

"I'm sorry I was late," she continued, speaking quickly, "but my mother took the car, and I thought she was going to come back in time, but by the time I realized she wasn't coming, it was too late, and . . ."

"That's fine," Robert said. "We didn't do anything. It's only the first night."

"All right, then," she said. "I'll see you next week."

"I hope so. Have a good night," he offered; she smiled and then was gone, the sound of her footsteps receding, leaving in the suddenly empty room, he thought, the faint, fragrance of perfume.

He gathered his belongings and walked down the hall

and out the door to where his bicycle, a tired, professorial three speed, was chained. He unlocked it, climbed wearily aboard, and pushed off on his three-mile ride back across the city.

Among the advantages of being an "adjunct"—defined by Robert's tattered paperback dictionary as "something added to another thing, but not necessarily a part of it"—was that he came and went as he pleased, taught his courses and then snuck off without partaking of the dreary machinations of academic life: discreet whispered words in the hallway, subtle internal jousting for status and power, and whatever other means academics used to derive their sense of self-worth. Among the disadvantages was that he was underpaid and overworked, ignored by his "boss" and colleagues alike, and worse yet, one day a week he taught at both the prestigious "Institute" and the community college in Slatters, on the other side of town—the side most White people he knew were scared of and had never been to. There was only an hour between his two classes, and if he wanted to eat between them he had to ride his bicycle swiftly, stop at a drugstore lunch counter, devour a quick hamburger, guzzle a tasteless cup of coffee, and press on the final mile or so to the college.

By the time class was over, it would be dark and he would retrace his path through the city, riding fast and with a not unpleasant sense of peril—past the "projects," over the trolley tracks, along the edge of the park, and then down again into the dimly lit city streets. It was a relief, after the careful solemnities and private aggravations of teaching—the speed, the darkness, the vague apprehension that someone would leap out of nowhere, tackle him, and drag him into the shadows.

As he crossed the river he could look out at the shimmering reflected lights of the Institute—a vast, sprawling array of buildings, constructed, as far as Robert could make out, entirely of poured concrete. His students there were overworked—so tired from studying that they routinely fell asleep during class, their heads tipping back against the seats like little dump trucks trying to empty themselves out. And when he passed his colleagues in the hall, they would utter a brief and pained hello and then look down and away, toward the wedge of shadow where the wall met the floor, where dust gathered and the fluff balls roamed. Why, he sometimes wondered, were these tenured professors made uneasy by a lowly adjunct like him? It was one of those jobs with no upward mobility—just a "glass ceiling" and a few "perks": free boxes of paper clips and lots of blue pens inscribed with the long, lofty title of the Institute. He could use the Xerox machine too, and shared an office with a kind and elderly Russian, a once famous linguist who now made a little extra money teaching writing to future scientists. Their classes were on different days, but once a term or so they would find themselves in the office at the same time, exchange pleasantries and farewells until the next semester. He felt at once for the old man a certain fondness, and also a fear that this was what he could become, minus the fame—a kindly, elderly adjunct, beloved and ignored and underpaid, living out the last of his days in the shadows of cinder-block walls, in the company of sleepy undergraduates with heads full of swirling, jostling numbers.

She sat in the front row on the left, next to a buffoonish young man with whom, it seemed to Robert, she rather openly flirted—bumping shoulders and sharing private jokes, her head tilting back when she laughed, revealing to him the pretty pink cavern of her mouth, guarded by the two white rows of her perfect teeth. She often wore, in the style of midwestern farmers, a white turtleneck and blue overalls, the knees of which had faded to a soft denim blue and impinged on his concentration as he sat and talked with other students, running on about term papers and footnotes and the importance of documenting sources and not plagiarizing, and other things in which he only halfheartedly believed. She wrote in the lovely cursive script of a schoolgirl, only a woman's version—not quite so big and loopy, and with less of a slant—and labored over her papers with a kind of serene intensity, pausing to stare up into a corner of the room, tapping her pencil on her barrette—sometimes pink, sometimes blue—before resuming. And then she, too, would come up for consultation, sit beside him as he went over her paper; she wrote well and made few grammatical errors, and so he found himself talking about other things—where she had grown up: Trinidad; how long she had been in this country: eleven years, since she was sixteen (eleven plus sixteen equals twenty-seven); where she had gotten her last name: "Italy—my grandfather was from there." She worked for a lawyer downtown, and had a boyfriend, he happened to know, for she had written about him in one of her papers: it was one of those "creative" assignments he learned about in graduate school (Write a "narrative" that begins with the four words "One hot summer night . . ."), and hers had described an evening when she and her boyfriend drove to the beach to swim. When they got there he had shed his clothes and gone dashing into the waves naked, but she, overcome by an unexpected shyness, had not followed and sat in the shadows on the sand, knees clasped to her breasts. He called out to her to join him, but she didn't, or couldn't, and when they got home he poked fun at her in front of their friends for being so prudish, and they had a fight from which, as far as Robert could make out, they had not yet recovered. The paper had moved him—the beach, the shadows, the intimation of nudity and of her brown and naked body, crouching shyly inside her clothes, refusing to come out. "Excellent paper," he had written at the bottom. "My only question, though; you never mention your boyfriend's name."

She was halfway back to her desk when she turned and said, with an amused laugh, "That's why I didn't write it. It's 'Robert,' like yours."

At the end of class she would often be the last to leave—she and the buffoonish young man, who, Robert gathered, sometimes gave her rides home; he could not help feeling envious as they left, bumping shoulders, and drifting out into the night in clouds of perfume and laughter—a collegiality from which he, in his role as teacher, was unfairly excluded. "Good night, Robert," she said as she passed through the doorway, smiling back at him with a look that evoked his first girlfriend, with whom he had fallen hopelessly in love and who had, consequently, ruined his entire sophomore year in college and subsequent summer, and then left him for a bearded teacher of "creative writing"—a subject Robert had thereafter hated and quietly refused to teach. But as he pushed off through the darkness and the cold October air, a round yellow moon rising up through the thinning leaves, the cold working its way into his knuckles and up his sleeves, it was the worn denim of her blue-jeaned knees that he remembered, the distracting fleck of gold in the iris of her eye as he tried to explain why a semicolon, and not a comma, should be used when connecting two independent clauses.

It was with such thoughts drifting through his head that he distractedly noticed, as he pedaled slowly through a housing project, two young boys standing furtively in a doorway, and as he rolled past he felt something hit him in the chest, and then heard it—a rock, a marble?—as it tumbled away across the pavement. He looked back in time to see one of the boys slip the slingshot under the coat, and he instinctively wheeled around and pedaled back toward them; but to his surprise they just stood there, staring dully back at him, daring him.

"Nice shot!" he half shouted, coming to a reluctant, re-

lieved stop, instantly aware of both the lameness of his remark and his own "otherness"—the paleness of his skin, the
rusting bicycle, the knit sweater and tweed jacket he was
wearing. He stared at them for a moment and tried to assume a more professorial stance. "You could put someone's
eye out!" he said, and then turned and rolled slowly away,
glancing back to see if they were laughing. Better to absorb
the blow than to threaten children—children who, he noticed, were not at all frightened of him, and might have a
room full of uncles inside looking for something to do. But
it was a good shot, he had to admit, a moving target at
twenty yards: had the slingshot been a bow and the rock an
arrow, it would have passed cleanly through the tweed of
his jacket, his faded blue cotton shirt, through flesh and
bone until it reached the soft, warm cushion of his heart.

By the time he got home it was after nine—time enough,
only, for a walk around the block, a beer purchased at the
local liquor store, and a slow, inevitable stroll back to his
solitary, drafty apartment, where, resigned to spending the
night alone, he would drink the beer in front of the grainy
black-and-white television set and then collapse onto a double bed, littered with books and magazines in lieu of another
person. He had been alone, girlfriendless, for nearly a year,
and had sort of adjusted to bachelorhood—lots of grilled
cheese sandwiches and cans of soup, late-night thumbing
through his address book looking for people to call. His
previous relationship had been an arduous one, and he had
resolved, at the end of it, to remain single for an entire solar
year, but now that the year was almost over there were no
likely prospects in sight. He had never been adept at "picking up" women—had not been blessed with that ineffable
combination of jocular indifference and sexual abandon to
which women, against their better judgment, were hopelessly
drawn; rather, he liked to imagine, he possessed a subtler,
slower kind of charm which needed, among other things, a

willing subject and time, and worked on them with a slow, oceanic persistence, like an endless succession of smallish waves washing onto a sandy, yielding shore. But lately, there had been no one, not even a kiss or the possibility of romantic adventure—only a beautiful woman in a coffee shop he sometimes went to, but he had not yet figured out how to get her out from behind the counter, out of her smock, and into a quiet, subterranean bistro where they could talk, hold hands, and then stroll back to his apartment for a night of ravenous lovemaking. Until then, it was more grilled cheese sandwiches and cans of soup, long nocturnal meanderings through the leafy streets of his neighborhood, hoping to run into someone he knew.

Among the other disadvantages of being an adjunct was that by the middle of the semester, he was tired: the endless procession of students, the papers that seemed to mate and reproduce inside his floppy briefcase, the shuttling back and forth on his bike. At the Institute he was corralled, each term, to help judge the "writing contest," wading through yet another, taller stack of papers, trying to find among them several worthy of a prize. He didn't mind the reading, so much, but he was then obliged to meet with three of his colleagues in one of their tiny cement cubicles and mull over the possibilities, locked in muted debate until, finally, the most persistent remained, the exhausted others relented, and the "decision" was made. At first, it had seemed that judging the contest was some kind of honor being bestowed on him, promise of future rewards, but after two or three years he had noticed that none of his fellow judges were real "professors" either; none were the tenured people who taught only one course a term and wrote books that were read only by each other, and jousted for status and power and conspired to keep Robert from rising from his lowly status into anything resembling a real job. The honor of judging the writing contest, it had slowly dawned on him, always fell to adjuncts like him. At the awards luncheon he had to stand up and announce the winners of one of the prizes—a few amusing words, something about how hard it was to judge, and then, with a certain gravity, the names of the winners, handshakes, a kiss for the girls, and he was done, his face burning, his body sweating lightly inside his cotton shirt. And when it was over, the last prize given, the few glowing winners huddled around their mentors and the disappointed others skulking back to their rooms, he, too, snuck away— down the hall to his bicycle, which he pedaled tiredly home, the vast, gray weight of the place receding behind him.

He reached his apartment in time to hear the telephone ringing, left the key in the door and ran, and caught it on the fourth ring. He didn't recognize the voice at first—soft and shy and familiar, but from where? "Sorry to bother you at home," a woman said, "but I was looking for the books for the research paper, and I couldn't find them in the library, and I was wondering, if I gave you the names of the authors, could you look for me at that other college where you teach, if it's not too much trouble?" She had blurted it out all at once, and by the time she finished he had figured out who it was.

"Hi, Maria," he said. "I didn't recognize your voice at first."

"After all these weeks? That hurts. Anyway, can you help me?"

"Probably." He was trying to slow himself down. "How did you get my number?"

"You gave it to us—at the beginning of the semester, re-member?"

"Not really, but that's okay. What are the names of the books?"

She told him, and the following morning he found them with comical ease in the cavernous stacks at the Institute. That night he looked for her number on the attendance sheet he had passed around on the first night of class, but to his displeasure it wasn't there: she had come in late. Panicked, he rifled through the phone book, found "Marcano," and called four of the seven listed numbers before he found himself talking to a woman with a strong West Indian accent: "Just a moment," the woman said, and a moment later Maria came on the line, her voice shy and liquid, as though she had just woken up from a nap. He had found the books, he told her and would bring them to class the following week; she wanted them sooner. "Can you meet me somewhere?" He felt something shift, like ballast, near the center of his chest.

"That would be fine." He spoke slowly, mind racing, and agreed to meet her at a coffee and croissant emporium not far from his house.

It was an ash gray Saturday, leaden and overcast and Novemberlike. He had arrived early and she was late, and by the time he saw her outside, leaning on a leafless tree, her head swaying to the unheard sounds of a yellow Walkman, he was heavily caffeinated and anxious and half convinced she would not come. He walked quickly, afraid she would disappear before he reached her, and offered to buy her a coffee, and they went inside, into a glassy atrium, and sat at a Parisian-style table next to a leafy ficus tree. They sat for an hour talking, not about her term paper, but about her grandmother in Trinidad; the music she had been listening to on her Walkman; her job as an assistant to a lawyer downtown; her boyfriend also named Robert with whom she had made some kind of truce, but whom, in the wake of the nude swimming incident, she was keeping at arm's length. "And what about you?" she said, listing toward him. "Where's *your* girlfriend?"

"Don't have one," he was pleased to report. "Not for a year or so."

"But you're looking, right?" She stared at him with soft, questioning eyes.

"Not really."

"Men are always looking," she said. "Even when they're married—*especially* when they're married."

She was speaking from experience, he suspected, but did not press it, and steered the conversation back onto safer ground. He told her about getting shot by the slingshot after class, and this, too, amused her. "This is where he got me," he offered, pointing to the spot on his rib cage, but she remained unimpressed.

"I think you'll make it," she said, and looked at him with a long, steady gaze.

"Well, I better go," he said.

"You don't like talking to me?" she said slowly, folding and refolding her napkin with her smooth, slender fingers. She knew she had him hooked.

"No, I do. I'm just supposed to go to someone's house for dinner." Why was he lying?

"A girl's?" she asked, her face framed among the ficus leaves. "No sir. Just kidding."

By the time they left it was almost dark; he walked her to the bus stop and there handed over the four books, trying to invest in the transfer of weight, from his arms to hers, some intimation of something, but what? The back of his hand touched the cool leather jacket; the gray and coldness seemed to press around them; the bus appeared and rolled to a stop, kneeled before her. "Thanks for meeting me," she said, turning her smile on him one last time, climbing onto the bus like a high school girl, books clasped to her breast, and then she was gone, and Robert was walking slowly through the gathering gloom, in the vague direction of home.

One of the further advantages of being an adjunct, perhaps, was that these unspoken boundaries, these dusty mores of student-teacher relations, did not fully apply to him, or applied in the same diminished proportion as his pay to that of a full-time professor's. In any case, she was twenty-seven—"a perfect cube," he had pointed out, three to the power of three—only four years younger than he. She was beautiful, and evoked his college heartthrob—beautiful teeth, the same open gaze she liked to turn on vulnerable men without thinking much of the consequences. But he was older now, and wiser, better equipped to keep her at a safe and academic remove.

The last few weeks of class were taken up with rather frantic talk of note taking and footnotes and visits to the library and warnings about plagiarizing, and the general repetition of things, it seemed to him, he had said one thousand times before. He was tired, tireder still, but his eagerness for the term to be over was tempered by his desire that it never end, that she continue to sit there, front row on his left, dutifully working on her papers, coming up to discuss them, knocking his knees underneath the table. One night she did not appear at all, and as he stood in front of the room, rambling on about paraphrasing, he was overcome by a sudden, enormous heaviness, an overwhelming lack of interest in what he was saying, and it was the best he could do not to dismiss the class an hour early and go home and call her; and in the end, he did let out the class fifteen minutes early, drove home, bolstered himself with a beer, found her number in his briefcase, paused, steadied himself, and dialed. "She's not home, dear," her mother said sympathetically. "Who's calling?"

"Oh, just her teacher," Robert confessed. "I just wanted to tell her the assignment. I'll try again tomorrow."

"All right, dear," she said, and hung up. He went out for a long, sobering walk, and when he came home and slept, but poorly, she appeared in his dreams—white turtleneck, overalls, high forehead, her brown and beautiful face. Where was she, on this, a class night? The imagined visage of her boyfriend came into view. He recognized his symptoms, and the following day he tried to press her from his mind, but couldn't. That evening, he resisted calling again, distracted himself by going to a bar and drinking too much, and by the time he got home it was too late to call. By the next morning he had half forgotten her, or at least was thinking of her for only half the time, and then it was almost the weekend: in two or three days, he would see her in class anyway, and soon the term would be over, and she would recede like the hundreds of students before her.

As emblematic of this change in outlook, the next morning he took his eggs scrambled, not fried, and ate them with a pleasant sense of liberation, of having freed himself from a tight and thickening plot. He read the paper slowly, planned his day—laundry, lunch, a movie, a run by the river, and a beer or two with a friend, if he could find one—a day mercifully devoid of romantic preoccupation. He indulged himself in a second coffee, and walked slowly home along a pavement nicely mottled by a warm late-November rain, feeling strangely happy, nearly euphoric with his newfound strength. He was halfway up the stairs when he heard the phone ringing, and he ran, fumbling with the key, darting in, the door swinging shut behind him.

"Did I wake you?" she asked. Her voice was softer this time, almost inaudible.

"Not at all." He could feel his heart beating from his run, and all the hard work of the week dissolving in one long, slow-moving instant, like an aspirin dropped into a warm and salty sea. "I just ran up the stairs," he said, catching his breath. "Where are you?"

"Home," she said, and then added, in the cadence of a question, "but I'm going out soon, if you want to meet."

He loitered all morning and half the afternoon, unable to do the things he had planned, and instead wandered through the streets of the city in the general direction of the coffee and croissant emporium where they had met a few weeks before. It was she who was early this time, and in the absence of pedagogical pretense, shy, and they walked in silence toward the Chinese restaurant she had suggested, through the teeming masses of Saturday shoppers, and then into the pleasant yellow room of the restaurant, where, oddly, they were the only diners. "Sorry I couldn't come to class last week," she said. "My father told me I could use the car, but then he changed his mind, and it was too late to take the train."

"That's fine," Robert said. "I almost called you that night, but I didn't dare. Actually, that's a lie: I did call, and spoke to your mother, but then didn't want to call back."

"You should have," she said, watching her own fingers as they fiddled with her chopsticks. "I've never been able to use these. Do you know how?"

He reached across the table and showed her, arranging them in her fingers, showing her how the thumb and forefinger worked in collusion to induce a gentle, scissoring motion. Tea came, then food. She ate chicken wings, he pork fried rice.

"So why didn't you call back?" she asked.

"I didn't want your mother to think badly of me. She might not like it."

"I'm twenty-seven years old!"

"Teachers aren't supposed to call their students very often."

"Whyyy?" she protested. "We're friends, aren't we?"

"I think so, but . . ."

"Do you?" she asked, baiting him, trying to get him to say things he wouldn't ordinarily dare. She spoke softly. "You've never had a student for a friend?"

"Not really," he said.

"Do you mind?"

"No—not at all."

"We can still be friends when the class is over, can't we?" Her wide brown eyes were looking straight at him, and she was wearing a button-down shirt, and when she leaned forward the cloth parted to reveal the swelling of her breasts.

He swallowed, feeling weak. "I hope so." He followed the lines of her collarbone to her neck, her chin, her lips. She wore no lipstick. "What kind of friends?" he asked, looked briefly into the eyes, at the fleck of gold.

"Whatever." She shrugged, and then, after a longish, lingering pause, added, "Can't I look into your beautiful blue eyes?"

He said nothing and then feebly offered, "Of course."

"You don't want me to?"

"I do. It's just hard to look back."

"Why?" she protested. "There's nothing wrong in it."

"I know. . . . You're too beautiful, that's all."

This, finally, was too much for even her, and she did look away, down across the table at the ruin of their meal—her unfinished chicken, a disemboweled egg roll, a cooling pot of tea.

"You think so?"

"Yes—don't you?"

"I'm okay, I guess," she said, in the classical understatement of beautiful women. "Nothing special."

"Your boyfriend thinks so," he said.

"No, he doesn't," she said. "He's not really my boyfriend, anyway."

"No?"

"Not this week, anyway." She glanced down at her watch. "He's an ass." The mention of him was a mistake, he now realized, and had broken the spell. "Should we go soon?" she said. "I have to get the bus back."

He helped her on with her coat, paid, and followed her back across the room and out. It was a relief to be outside again, and not have to look at her eyes, or keep up with the bantering, dangerous pace of her conversation. He walked a half step behind her, and as they crossed the street he lightly took her arm, and then released it. They strolled across the campus of the college and back again, and had almost reached the bus station when she asked, so softly he almost did not hear, "Do you like music?"

"Most music. Why?"

"I have some tickets to a concert," she said, "and I was wondering if you want to go. But, I think it's the last night of class."

"Who is it?" he asked, trying to take the invitation in stride.

"I'm not sure—I won the tickets at work."

"I think I could—we usually just have a party on the last night." They had reached the bus stop, and their walk had slowed to a crawl. "But we can get out early, proba-bly."

"Well, let me know if you want to go," she said, "so I don't ask somebody else."

"Don't do that—I'll go," he blurted out, and he was go-ing to say something else but the bus hissed to a stop, and she turned to board it.

"Aren't you going to say good-bye?" he said, and with-out a word she stopped, turned back toward him, and, with her eyes half closed, moved her face in proximity to his and kissed him, flush on the lips, as soft as a pillow, then was gone. Weightless, Robert turned and drifted back in the direction from which he had come.

In the days to follow he observed himself from a distance, and a small height, like the out-of-body experiences of those who have almost died and can see themselves below, on the operating table, as they drift upward toward the corridor of white light: from this vantage point he saw himself, aged thirty-one, walking the city streets, watching the faces of passing strangers as they moved through the reddish glow of Christmas lights, the cold crowding around them, the banal jingle of Christmas carols floating out from the storefront windows. *Can't I look into your beautiful blue eyes?* Had she actually said this? It seemed hard to believe, like something she had said in a dream and in his feeble state he had superimposed on the dinner in the Chinese restaurant. And had she turned to him, and kissed him, fully on the lips? The cloudlike softness of the kiss had stayed with him and haunted his sleep at night. In a week or two, it would all be over: Would he ever see her again, or would she disappear, like his other students, march off over the horizon and disappear forever? He had intended to see her—had called her once, twice, but had managed only to speak with her mother and left a message. For the first time in his life he bought an answering machine, but he returned to his apartment to find the light not blinking, but burning through the darkness with a steady, malevolent glow. But he *would* see her, at the very least at the class party, and then the concert she had invited him to, and the dull workings of his imagination began to list toward this event in an unhealthy hopefulness. Her grade would be final then, burnished into his grade book forever, and all ethical apprehensions would disappear.

But on the morning of his last class she called with bad news. "I can't get the car," she said, almost in a whisper. "My father took it to Connecticut without telling me. I don't know if he'll be back in time."

"You can't?" Robert said, quietly panicking. "Maybe I can call my sister." He did, and she agreed to loan him for the evening her aged, orange VW "Superbeetle" which, despite its sixteen years and several minor defects, worked; he called Maria back, and in the same hushed, conspiratorial tones, told her the good news.

"All right," she said. "I'll see you in class, then?"

"Yup."

The Volkswagen, Robert discovered, did indeed run, but the muffler seemed broken or incomplete, and as he drove the car growled like a small helicopter, and when he made turns to the left, something in the steering column caused some unseen wires to twist and touch, and the horn would honk, and he developed the tactic of turning very sharply and, when it honked, waving to imaginary friends. On his way to class he stopped at the liquor store to buy his own contribution to the party—two bottles of wine, a corkscrew, and a bag of garlic potato chips. He was nervous, less for the party than the concert—or rather, the fear that word would leak out that he was going to an after-class function with one of his students. But it was she who had asked him, he reminded himself, and who was he to say no?

There was always something oddly, unexpectedly stressful about these term-ending events—the enormous family-sized bottles of soda pop, potato chips, the scratchy music someone had brought on a tiny cassette, the novelty of having no other reason for being in the room than enjoying each other's company. Robert would find himself in the role of host, drifting around and trying to exchange pleasantries with all the students, even those he knew, in some secret, dark corner of his brain, would receive a D or worse. But this time things went smoothly, and the party even seemed to take off, in its way. There were a few wine drinkers besides Robert, and some of the shy, retiring men with grammatical problems emerged as womanizers, and Maria had assumed the role of first lady of the class, passing out food, refilling glasses, organizing group photos with the camera someone had brought. She danced, too, right there in the classroom, with a thin, lithe man from northern South America somewhere, for whom Robert felt a sudden antipathy; he was dancing closely, slyly, and made several attempts to hold her by the waist, but she held him off. Later, he saw them talking together in a corner of the room, and then saw her jot something down on a scrap of paper and hand it to him, and in Robert's mind his grade silently slipped, without fanfare, from a B to a C. More food appeared, a tray of fried chicken, a bowl of beans and rice, and Robert made the rounds, talking to each of his students, wishing them well, sipping wine and out of the corner of his eye watching the clock, half wishing they would all start to trickle out the door toward home. More people danced, and he was beckoned to the floor, but he begged off and, emboldened by wine, joked, "White people can't dance." He laughed, and then, as if to disprove himself, he was dancing, not with Maria, but with a plumpish middle-aged woman from Costa Rica who had attended class about half the time—Velma, he thought her name was. Maybe he couldn't fail her after all. "Mr. Robert," she joked when the song was over, "I had no idea! You got moves!"

And then the food was almost finished, and they started to leave, the men giving him a manly handshake, and the women offering their half-turned cheeks, Maria rounding up the plates and cups and packing up the remaining food and pressing them out the door with departing students. Then he, too, was walking out the door, with Maria and the buffoonish young man who had hopes, Robert guessed, of giving her a ride home. But she said something to him that he could not hear, and when they got to the door, he shook Robert's hand, looked Maria in the eye, and said, "I'll call you," and then he was gone, and with a suppressed sensation of triumph and possibility Robert was walking out into the darkness himself, her warm conspiratorial weight moving along beside him toward the crouching orange shape of the car.

Their seats were halfway up a steep, clifflike slope at the back of the arena, and in the distance they could see a

sequined beauty as she drifted around the stage in a cone of
yellow light, belting out a succession of love songs Robert
vaguely recognized from the jukebox of a bar he sometimes
went to after class; Maria knew every song, and leaned forward in her seat, lost in herself, mouthing the words, leaving Robert to listen on his own and study the side of her
half-turned face, her neck, her slowly moving lips, the arc
of her back he wanted to reach out toward and let his hand
settle on, but he did not dare: for in leaning forward she
had moved away from him, into the music and her own
past, formed with her back a kind of parenthesis, protect-
ing herself, and did not invite him in. For Robert, in his
weakened state, still woozy from wine and desire and ex-
haustion from the semester, the songs were too much, washing over him with their lilting cadences and melancholy
resolutions: loves that almost were but weren't, loves that
were but should not have been, loves that should have been
but weren't. For a moment, he dared himself to hold his
hand above her back, an inch, or two, felt the warmth rising from her like the heat from the sidewalk after a long
summer day, and another time he let his arm slide off the
armrest into her space, in a dark hollow of warmth formed
by the inward sway of her body above her hip, her waist.
Was that her he was touching, or a fold in her clothing? But
then she moved, in such a way that seemed to indicate that
was enough of that experiment, and he moved his arm back
into its own space.

At one point she turned back to him and asked, above
the sound of the music, "Do you like it?" but when he nodded
yes and then leaned toward her to say something else, she
smiled and turned back toward the stage, where the sequined
beauty had been joined by a barrel-shaped man in a tuxedo
named Luther, who sang in a deep, liquid baritone and, at
the end of one song, held the woman in his arms and, to a
triumphant avalanche of applause, leaned over and kissed

her. But as the alcohol seeped out of him, and the songs washed over him, her hopeless proximity wore him down, and he wanted to get out—away from these swooning people and her smooth and beautiful back and the fringes of frizzled hair that shone in the glow of the distant lights. He remembered the kiss, the hour or two they had passed in the Chinese restaurant, the way she had said, "Can't I look into your beautiful blue eyes?" Why had she actually said this? What had changed? Now that the semester was over, and they were no longer protected by the cocoon of the class, she knew she had to draw her own boundaries, circle the wagons against whatever it was she had stirred up in him. The sadness of the music, perhaps, had brought back some hurt in her, pulled her back into herself. Whatever they had shared back in the Chinese restaurant, on their walk afterward, in the kiss at the bus station, was, as they said in high school, "history."

"Did you like it?" she asked again as they moved along with the throng, down the ramps of the arena and out into the cold December air.

"Of course . . ." he said, but could muster no further elaboration and instead took her arm, held it to his side even after his fingers had turned numb with cold. Through the leather he could feel the cushion of her arm, but it was unyielding, dead to him, and invited no further advances. "The term is over, finally," he offered.

"Thank God!" she said, and then added, with a glance, "No offense, I mean, I enjoyed it. I'm just tired."

He didn't know this part of the city, and as he drove she gave directions, guiding him back through the neighborhood, along a route that involved a lot of left-hand turns, and whenever he made one the horn would honk, and he would feign a wave to a passing car, but the novelty had passed and she no longer laughed.

"Your mother will be waiting up," he said.

"She knows better," she said, looking out the window, out onto the passing lights.

"So we're still going to be friends, right?" he ventured.

"Of course—why wouldn't we?" Her tone was flat, matter-of-fact.

"Thanks for the concert—it was nice. Too many love songs, though."

"What's wrong with love songs?" she protested, and for a moment it was back—that lilting, flirtatious cadence to her voice, a lightness he had not heard since the party.

"Nothing, really—they're just hard to listen to, sometimes. That's all." He had hoped she would ask him why, so he could confess his problem to her, his love, but she didn't.

"That's true."

He tried to read in the two words some other, hidden meaning, but couldn't make it out. She was looking out the window again, her forehead pressed to the glass. "I'm tired," she said softly.

"When should I call you?"

"Whenever. It's right up here—the brown house at the end of the block."

"Are your parents home?" he asked, clinging to the receding hope that the evening would not end here, that she would invite him in and they could sit for an hour and talk, and then, in parting, he could kiss her again on the lips and hold her for a minute, in the understanding that she would have liked to invite him onto the bed he had so often imagined, but, for reasons hardly worth articulating, couldn't.

"It's here," she repeated, with a trace of urgency, as if he might miss it. Robert slowed and pulled up, cut the engine, and then glided a little way beyond the house in the final hope that she would at least linger for a moment, sit with him for a moment or two in the warm pocket of the car and talk, leave things open for the future.

Instead, he heard the door handle click, felt the cold air

rushing in, and she was halfway outside when, in one final act of desperation he reached out toward her but managed only to touch her hair, running through his fingers like silk, then her shoulder as she got quickly out outside, looking back in.

"Maria—I have a terrible crush on you," he blurted out. "I can't help it." He looked up at her as she stood in the frame of the doorway, and then down at his feet. "I'm sorry—I just don't know what to do about it." He half hoped she would get back into the car to discuss his confession, but she knew better, and stood there looking back in, confused.

"I just had to tell you, that's all," he added.

She looked wistful, and smiled in sympathy. "You'll be all right. Call me," she said, finally, but there was a pleading quality in her voice, as if what she was really saying was something closer to "Don't call me, please. The semester is over. This will never work. Thanks for a great semester!"

"I will," he said, but he also knew that the moment of possibility had passed, and would never return. She had weighed it all out already, and made up her mind.

"Call me," she repeated weakly.

"I will. And thanks for the concert." He was trying to let her go, but then couldn't, quite. "Wait—how will you get your paper back?"

"Mail it," she said. "Or leave it in your box. I'll pick it up sometime—it doesn't matter. I think I have a copy." He couldn't blame her for this final cruelty—he had asked for it.

"All right, then. Good night. Thanks again."

"Good night, Robert."

The door shut, and he watched as she went quickly up the steps, heard the lock to her house click open and then closed, locked, sealing her in.

He pulled away quickly, clumping down over the curb with another accidental honk, made a U-turn, and headed back toward the malevolent orange glow of the city.

His face was still flushed and the ends of his fingers tingled where they had touched her hair. Beside him, the seat where she had been sitting was still warm. He pressed it with his hand. "Call me," she had said, but with a pained, unfamiliar quality in her voice, and he knew enough of women to know that the corner had been turned, the threshold reached but not crossed, and he also knew that his troubles were not over, that whatever it was she had opened up in him would not go away on its own, nor disappear with the A he would be giving her, that she deserved. It was all strangely familiar, for she had jostled loose in him some painful lesson from his past, but what was it? She had left a clue or two—a lock of hair, the warmth on the seat beside him, the fading fragrance of her which, even now, he could not quite remember—but the true meaning of what had happened hovered in the middle distance, a mirage, just beyond reach.

Who would help him now? No one: like all good teachers, she had left him to find the answers for himself.